"Want to dance with me?" Yasmine asked

Alex agreed, even though he didn't really want to. But he loved the idea of watching her dance, and moments later that's exactly what he was doing. Yasmine's moves were even hotter than he'd imagined. Mesmerized by the sway of her hips, he forgot about everyone else in the room.

They danced through song after song before a slow one came on, and they m____ closer together. Her hands slid up his ____ ____ his neck.

Their first real physical co____

Her body pressed agains____ ____ he slow beat of the music ____ an intimate dance with ____ ____ching more. He wanted h____ ____ it, no ignoring it for a sec____ ____ouldn't let him. And she couldn't h____ ____ow it, too.

Then she did something unexpected. She pressed her abdomen more firmly against him. Her gaze sparked with daring.

"I've got a thing for you," she whispered into his ear. "And I think we need to do something about it."

Dear Reader,

Don't we all want to be desired more than anything by another person? In *Any Way You Want Me,* Yasmine Talbot has both the fortune and misfortune of being the object of many men's desire. It may sound like an enviable position, but Yasmine knows all too well the disadvantages of men becoming too enamored with her appearance and never seeing the person within. When her past—and two men from it—comes back to haunt her, she'll discover that it's possible for love to grow from the darkest moments in her life, and that sometimes being wanted isn't such a bad thing.

I hope you enjoy Yasmine and Alex's story as much as I loved bringing it to life. Visit my Web site, www.jamiesobrato.com, for monthly contests, new release updates and more.

Sincerely,

Jamie Sobrato

Books by Jamie Sobrato

HARLEQUIN BLAZE

HARLEQUIN TEMPTATION

ANY WAY YOU WANT ME

Jamie Sobrato

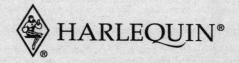

TORONTO • NEW YORK • LONDON
AMSTERDAM • PARIS • SYDNEY • HAMBURG
STOCKHOLM • ATHENS • TOKYO • MILAN • MADRID
PRAGUE • WARSAW • BUDAPEST • AUCKLAND

To my family near and far,
for all your love and support

ISBN 0-373-79220-4

ANY WAY YOU WANT ME

Copyright © 2005 by Jamie Sobrato.

This edition published by arrangement with Harlequin Books S.A.

® and TM are trademarks of the publisher. Trademarks indicated with
® are registered in the United States Patent and Trademark Office, the
Canadian Trade Marks Office and in other countries.

www.eHarlequin.com

Printed in U.S.A.

Prologue

FOR TEN YEARS he had been watching her.

The watching had started out as a niggling fascination with her beauty and notoriety, a game to see if he could keep up with her life, her whereabouts. But later she'd haunted his dreams to the point that he'd tried to put her out of his head.

He'd tried, but the game was addictive.

Now he wanted more. He wanted her. Not just to satisfy the physical desires—though that need could not be denied—but also for her skills. She could give him the access he needed to the information he wanted—highly valuable information that would be his ticket out of the rat race and in to a place in the Caymens.

She was a worthy opponent, and she would be a worthy partner.

There had been rules for the game he'd played with himself. He could look but he could not touch. He could have her only in his fantasies, where she remained delicious and perfect, unsullied by disappointing reality. And for ten years that had been enough.

But this was his game, and now he would change the rules.

1

THE NEW GUY in the office was a serious distraction.

How was a girl supposed to concentrate when there was a six-foot-tall specimen of male perfection strutting around, on his way to the copy machine, the fax machine, the coffee maker—always on his way somewhere, and always passing by Yasmine Talbot's desk.

As he walked by just now, his ocean-and-evergreen scent wafting over her, Yasmine's fingers halted on the keyboard, and when he was well past her desk, she turned to watch. Two days ago, she'd nearly fallen out of her chair watching.

He knew the effect he was having on her, and he probably reveled in his power. From the moment they'd first laid eyes on each other last week when he'd emerged from the new-employee training session and stood across the room from her, blinking under the fluorescent lights, they'd begun a silent office flirtation that had gotten progressively bolder by the day. Now it bordered on the ridiculous that they'd yet to even say hello to each other, even in an office as big as VirtualActive's. Were they just going to exchange hot-and-heavy glances forever?

Yasmine was both amused and embarrassed by the animal-mating-dance quality their relationship had assumed. She imagined them starring in their own Discovery Channel documentary—Mating Habits of the Common Office Drone. He fluffed his feathers, strutted to and fro, made searing eye contact. Essentially he was staking his claim. But Yasmine didn't want to be claimed. Nor did she want to star in any mating-ritual documentaries in the midst of her workplace. And yet she couldn't deny how mesmerized she was by him. It was as if she'd been biologically programmed to want him.

This guy, with his windswept hair and his perfect ass, was the stuff heroes on the covers of romance novels were made of. Put him in a billowing white shirt unbuttoned to reveal his chest, with a beautiful damsel draped on one arm, and he'd look right at home. But put him in the middle of the mundane offices of VirtualActive, Inc. and he was likely to spawn his own interactive sex game, Virtual Alpha Male. And don't think that, as the only female programmer at the sex software company, she hadn't seriously considered it.

In fact, she realized, as she glanced at the file full of notes on her latest software project, Sexcapade, a night with a guy like him probably was just what she needed to kick-start her creativity. So far, she'd been uninspired, and the project was going badly.

But her attraction to the new guy was slightly bizarre. She didn't do beefed-up, all-American-surfer-boy types. She was completely immune to the charms of calendar hunks with too-perfect hair. Yet here she was, her girl parts getting all tingly every time this guy who was prettier than she was strolled by. It had to be the lack of available attractive men in her life.

Her type of guy was darker, more brooding, prone to

motorcycles and leather. True, she had a bad-boy fixation—particularly if they were the unattainable, strictly fantasy type. But the way she figured, bad boys and bad girls went hand in hand. Yasmine might have turned pretending to be good into an art form, but in her heart lurked a rebel.

The new guy disappeared into the break room, and Yasmine tried to turn her attention back to her work. But her mind kept wandering.

One other problem with him—he looked as though he belonged in L.A. more than San Francisco. He had a *tan,* for crying out loud.

Where would anyone, especially a programmer who spent his days attached to a computer, even get a tan in this city in the middle of December? The answer was he wouldn't, not unless he was going to a tanning bed—did those even exist anymore?—which this guy must have been doing. A fact that should have repulsed Yasmine.

Instead, she found herself wondering if he had tan lines. One of her more disturbingly detailed fantasies even had her freeing him of his khakis, inch by inch, to discover not a single line. It was ridiculous. He was probably the kind of guy who had a Playboy bunny tattoo right next to his schlong.

The break room door opened, and the object of her whacked fantasies came out carrying a bottle of Evian water. She watched him walk to the printer, his snug pants advertising the well-sculpted muscles beneath them, and shook her head. It was official—Yasmine was losing her freaking mind.

She glared at her computer screen and promised herself she would do no more ogling today. She would focus on her work. Focus, focus, focus.

If only he *looked* like any other code-slinging brainiac who spent too much time indoors and could use a trip to the nearest fashion consultant, there would be no problem. But he didn't. And he worked in her office, no less. Yasmine didn't do the office help. So she took her tingly feelings as a sign that she'd spent a few months too many sans boyfriend.

She just needed to get laid, and she'd stop drooling over her strutting, preening office mate.

"Excuse me," she heard an unfamiliar male voice say.

Yasmine looked up to see the object of her constant ogling looming beside her desk. He smiled faintly, his gaze locked on her. She opened her mouth to say hi, but nothing came out.

"Is this yours?"

She stared at the document she'd printed an hour ago and nodded. "I, um, I…forgot to go pick it up."

He placed it on top of her in-box pile and smiled. He had perfect white teeth. "We should stop this, don't you think?"

"Stop what?"

"Staring at each other but never talking."

Staring? Had she been staring?

"We're talking now," she said stupidly.

"I'm Kyle Kramer," he said.

She liked his voice…and his eyes, which were a smoky shade of hazel. They were mesmerizing—almost unreal looking.

"Hi, Kyle Kramer," she croaked.

And now that he'd formally introduced himself,

would it be forward to take him home and have her way with him?

Definitely she should at least tell him her name first. She pointed to the nameplate on her cubicle wall. "That's me. Yasmine."

If her conversational skills got any more brilliant, she'd have to shoot herself.

He smiled and nodded. He had sort of a Rhett Butler attitude going on, as if he knew he was gorgeous enough to make most women feel that they could never fill Scarlet's shoes.

"Right," he said. *"Yaz-meen.* I've been pronouncing it wrong in my head."

So he'd been thinking about her? Had he maybe even been as distracted by overwrought office lust as she had? Very intriguing.

There was an awkward pause.

He studied the Christmas decorations all around her cubical, and it struck her as odd for the first time that she'd bothered to decorate her work space but not her home. Funky little ornaments she'd found at a shop in Noe Valley—a beaded green frog, a purple feather angel, a little carved wooden genie emerging from a bottle, a sparkly pink bird, among other things—hung from twinkling red lights around the top edge of the cubicle walls.

"Nice frog," he said, his tone almost languorous, as if he had no intention of leaving anytime soon.

"Is there, um, something I can help you with?"

She sounded like an uptight bitch, but she was unnerved by his unexpected presence, his seeming awareness of his effect on her.

"Would you maybe like to go for drinks after work?"

Drinks, dancing, hot, sweaty sex. She was game. But Yasmine knew better than to follow such wild impulses. In fact, she never followed them. She knew the right thing to do, the safe thing, would be to end this silly mating ritual right here, right now.

"I'm sorry—I have plans with a friend after work." Which was true.

He rested his forearms on top of her cubical wall and shrugged. "Okay, how about another night?"

"I've been working late most nights," she said, making herself sound like the workaholic she was.

He gave her a look that said he wasn't buying her excuses. "Going to the holiday party on Friday?"

Urgh, the annual office party. Only four days away. VirtualActive threw it at the same inconvenient time every year—the day before Christmas Eve—to kick off the holidays.

"I don't usually date office mates," she blurted. Idiot, idiot, idiot.

What was she so afraid of? Why did she have to play it too far on the safe side all the time?

He wasn't anyone she worked closely with…. And the upcoming holidays did have her feeling lonely…. And she had been feeling the urge to do something a tiny bit wild—maybe even something that could remind her what hot guys and hot passion were all about. And Kyle *did* make her squirm like no guy had in God knows how long.

"We'd just be going to the party together. It's hardly even a date."

Yasmine recalled last year's party, when Larry Mono-Brow Harris had gotten drunk and spent the entire night coming on to her. She shuddered. Maybe having a date wouldn't be such a bad idea.

"Well, I guess it's okay. Since you're new, I wouldn't want you to feel like an outcast for all the merriment." Yasmine smiled, and a weight she hadn't even noticed was lifted from her shoulders.

"We'll just call you my ambassador for the evening. I'll pick you up at six o'clock Friday night, then?"

And if he turned out to be a nutcase, she'd have to move to a new apartment. "As your ambassador, I should give *you* a ride to the party."

"Fair enough."

He stepped into her cubical, invading her professional space and making her dizzy with his too-large presence. As if he understood his effect on her, he glanced at her and smiled, then took a pen from her desk and began writing something on her memo pad. This close, the sheer weight of him became his most obvious and overwhelming attribute.

Yasmine had always found some irresistible lure in the size and weight of men. Their solidity. Their strength. It was the quality she was trying to convey in the male character for the Sexcapade project, but so far her on-screen guy still looked kind of flat and boring.

It was a quality that was never more apparent than when a guy was naked against her, moving inside her, all that force and heft and power barely restrained—and hard to duplicate on a computer screen.

And if she kept up this line of thinking, she'd definitely end up doing something she would later regret. Like invite Kyle to be her own personal muse for the night.

When he finished writing, he handed her the paper

with directions to his house on it as Yasmine discreetly tried to wipe away the film of perspiration that had formed on her upper lip.

"I might need to be a little later than six," she said, doing a mental calculation of how long it would take her to navigate rush-hour traffic, go home and transform herself from office-boring to going-out fabulous, then drive to his house. "Maybe more like seven."

He shrugged. "Sounds good."

A sense of déjà vu struck Yasmine. Something about him seemed to resonate with her. Maybe in another time, another place, they'd passed on the street. Or maybe in another lifetime….

Perhaps that was the explanation for her insane attraction to him. In a past life, they'd been a couple of enamored yaks in the mountains of Nepal, doing what yaks did best. She winced at the image.

"I'll see you later, then," she said, smiling. As if she'd be able to do much else.

This was the moment when he should have vacated her cubical, but instead he lingered a little too long. Her senses went on alert, and the tingly feeling in her nether regions returned with a vengeance. Then he smiled, nodded and he was gone.

She was pathetic. Her life had gotten so dull, even obvious guys like Kyle Kramer could get her hot.

She had to do something about this attraction so she could get back to work. Maybe he'd turn out to be an airhead, or a toad, or a guy who ate with his mouth open. And if not, if he was as perfect as he looked…

She knew the deal. In that case, what she needed was

a little excitement, and a whole lot of sexual satisfaction. Then maybe she could shake all this misguided lust.

Or something like that.

She turned back to her computer, but out of the corner of her eye, she could see someone approaching. She glanced over and spotted Drew Everton stopping in her cubicle entrance, which was suddenly *the* place to see and be seen, apparently.

Drew, clad in a Santa hat, had been at VirtualActive for at least as long as Yasmine had, but unlike her, he'd taken some initiative. He'd moved from programmer to team leader to project manager, and while everyone liked to point out that Yasmine had the talent to do the same, she just didn't feel the drive. He was a hard worker and a nice guy.

"What's up?"

"Did I overhear you making a date with that Kyle guy for the holiday party?"

"What? Do you have my desk bugged or something?" Yasmine was conscious now that any number of her co-workers had probably witnessed her conversation with Kyle.

"No, I was in the next aisle. I couldn't help but hear."

"You and who else?"

"It's not a crime to date a co-worker, you know."

"I just don't want everyone looking at me and whispering," Yasmine said. She'd endured that as a teenager and vowed she'd never be the subject of any controversy big or small, again. It wasn't the easiest vow to live with.

"Yeah, well, I can understand that. I'll keep my lips sealed about the subject, if that helps."

"Thanks, but I guess there's no point. People will see

me with Kyle at the party, regardless. But really, I'm only going so he won't be the lone new guy."

Drew flashed a doubtful look at her. "Speaking of dates, I've got one of my own for the party, and I was hoping maybe you could chat her up a little, give me your opinion on her."

"Of course I will. Where'd you meet her?" Yasmine said, then tried hard to suppress a yawn. She'd been awakened last night by a heavy-breathing phone call that she'd quickly hung up on, but the bastard had called back again and again until she'd finally had to disconnect the phone.

He sighed. "Online dating service—and you know how all the previous matches have worked out."

"Maybe this one will be better," Yasmine said without sounding very convincing.

"Yeah, maybe."

"You know, I've got a friend I think would be perfect for you. She broke up with her last boyfriend recently, and I think she's past the rebound phase now…."

"Is she hot?"

"She's very hot. But, more important, she's a good person."

He shrugged. "Okay, so hook me up."

"I'll work on it, but in the meantime, I'll definitely scope out the dating service girl for you Friday night."

"Thanks. I'll see you there," he said, then wandered off.

Yasmine turned her attention back to the nightmare of a software patch she'd been working on all afternoon, but her brain had given up. This was nothing that couldn't wait until tomorrow, or the next day, or the next week.

At the thought of the long, empty Christmas holiday coming up, her chest developed a dull ache. Her traitorous parents would be taking off for their annual trip to Paris, right in the middle of the holidays, leaving her orphaned at the one and only time of year she'd prefer not to be. They'd been going to Paris for Christmas ever since she was a little girl, but lately, tagging along had lost its appeal, and just once she'd like them to be more interested in spending the holiday with her than with their favorite city in Europe.

All her friends would be spending time with their families, and she'd be sitting home alone, watching Christmas specials on TV and feeling sorry for herself. Some friends had invited her to their holiday gatherings, but she'd politely refused, not wanting to crash their family traditions.

So here she was, a few days before the Christmas weekend, with her only holiday plans being the annual office party, and her only sure companionship a guy she'd just met—a guy she was entertaining using for sexual inspiration.

How sad was that? Yasmine hated how alone she'd felt lately. Alone and strangely vulnerable. She suspected the feelings had started with the odd phone calls she'd occasionally been getting late at night. Sometimes silence, sometimes heavy breathing, sometimes even moans that sounded disturbingly like a guy coming on the other end of the line.

She'd reported the calls to the phone company, but they'd said there was nothing they could do unless she wanted to change her number. She'd opted for waiting to see if the calls stopped. So far, no luck.

They did make her more worried about the sense she sometimes got that she was being watched. But really, that feeling had been with her ever since her teen years, after she'd learned she was the object of an FBI investigation. Probably she was just being paranoid for no good reason.

Whatever the source of Yasmine's discontent, she was pretty damn sure Kyle could be a fun distraction.

SOON, IF HE WAS LUCKY, he'd find out the truth about Yasmine Talbot.

Alex DiCarlo, otherwise known as Kyle Kramer for the extent of his employment at VirtualActive, watched Yasmine from across the room. She stood up from her desk and walked down the aisle between two rows of cubicles, then disappeared out of the office. She was even prettier up close than she was from afar, and so much more a woman now than she'd been the first time he'd laid eyes on her over ten years ago.

Her long black hair hung nearly to her waist, glossy and straight. Her huge, baby-doll brown eyes belied the fact that she was a wild child, a woman who'd once spent a year in a youth correctional facility, while her skin, pale café au lait thanks to her Indian mother and her English father, was unbelievably flawless.

And she had a way of wearing tight clothes that could plant dirty thoughts in the head of a priest. Today, her black pants and stretchy red sweater had nearly made Alex forget the real reason he was watching her—not purely for her aesthetic appeal.

But there had always been that conflict inside him where Yasmine was concerned. The desire to see justice served versus the sexual desire she stirred in him. Years ago she'd been utterly forbidden, an underage teen and the subject of his investigation. He never would have acted on his attraction, never would have even admitted it existed—not even to himself. Now, though, she was a grown woman, and the temptation was much greater.

She didn't know he'd been watching her every move for the past two weeks—couldn't know—or that he knew all the details of her criminal past.

Most important, she couldn't find out his real identity. So far Yasmine hadn't shown any sign of recognizing him. Unless she'd illegally accessed employment files that showed his FBI photo, she hadn't laid eyes on him in nine years. Not since he'd testified against her in the trial that had sent her away to juvenile prison.

He'd gone to a hell of a lot of trouble to get close to Yasmine now—using old contacts to obtain a fake ID, fake job references, and he'd brushed up his slightly creaky programming skills.

He'd also changed his appearance to ensure she wouldn't recognize him. Six months of growing his hair had left him looking less like the FBI agent he no longer was and more like the obsessed surfer he was fast becoming. The tan he'd acquired from countless days on his surfboard added to the look, and the many hours he'd spent at the gym working out his career frustrations on the weight machines had taken his body from thin but fit to admirably bulky.

A pair of colored contact lenses had completed his transformation from clean-cut FBI agent Alex DiCarlo to California surfer Kyle Kramer.

Now all he had to do was get close enough to Yasmine to answer once and for all the question of whether or not she was still a hacker. But if he got close enough to find that out, would he then be too close to resist asking for more from her? She was the most beautiful woman he'd ever seen, and the most intriguing.

But he couldn't let that temptation deter him. He had to know the truth.

Then he'd be able to get the hell away from this tedious programming job and get on with what was left of his normal life. He may not have his career in the FBI to go back to, but he did have a fledgling information security business that he would never be able to get off the ground until he put this obsession with Yasmine's case behind him.

In the past two weeks he'd cultivated his programmer persona while settling into the new office, trying to be as inconspicuous as possible, and so far he'd been a success. With the technical skills he'd acquired while working to stop cybercriminals at the FBI's San Francisco field office, he blended right into the offices of VirtualActive, Inc.

But he wasn't sure how much more of this charade he could take. He hated lying to people, hated pretending to be someone he wasn't. He didn't want to be in this place deceiving an office full of basically decent people, even if it was for a good cause. He needed to get an in with Yasmine sooner rather than later.

Alex had to know the real reason he'd lost his FBI career, had to know if Yasmine had been involved, had to know if he'd caused his own downfall or if someone else had helped him out of his job.

His former partner, Ty Connelly, had been insistent that Yasmine was a major suspect in their investigation, and it only occurred to Alex recently to wonder about Ty's motives. Why had he been so adamant in the face of so little evidence?

Alex made a mental note to give Ty a call and meet him for drinks, where he could maybe pry some details about the investigation out of him. But he doubted it would uncover anything new. Ty was a good agent, a man Alex could trust.

Probably more so than he could trust his own judgment where Yasmine was concerned. That was his most compelling reason for pursuing the investigation on his own—he had to prove to himself that he could get to the truth. If he didn't, he would live with the doubts about his own competence for the rest of his life. He'd have to live with his own failure, and that was not acceptable.

Forcing his thoughts back to the task at hand, he skimmed the new e-mail messages in his in-box and was about to call it quits for the day when he heard someone clearing his throat behind him. He turned to see Drew Everton, still wearing the goofy Santa hat he'd been wearing all day, pulling his rolling desk chair across the aisle to park in Alex's cubicle.

"Hey man, congrats."

"About what?"

"Bagging a date with Yasmine. It's about time somebody besides Larry Harris got the nerve to ask her out."

Alex shrugged. "Thanks," he said, playing along.

And also hoping he could use this opportunity to acquire a bit of information. He'd gotten kind of buddy-buddy with Drew during the short time he'd been at

VirtualActive, but he'd yet to broach the subject of Yasmine because there'd never been an unobtrusive time to do so.

"So what can you tell me about her?" he asked, trying to sound casual.

"What's to tell? She's hot, she's intelligent, she's a programming genius."

"Is she that girl I remember seeing on the news way back when? The convicted hacker?"

Drew nodded. "One and the same."

"You think she's still into that stuff?"

"No way. I talked to her once about her trial and everything. She said she was finished with hacking, that she was afraid she was being watched all the time and couldn't imagine breaking the law again."

"You believe her?"

"Why wouldn't I? She'd be crazy to risk going back to jail," Drew said.

"Some hackers just can't give it up."

"I'd be surprised if she was that type. I think she was just a kid who got in way over her head, and she learned her lesson."

Maybe Drew was right. There was a part of Alex that wanted to believe that of her, wanted to stop the investigation now. But the bigger part of him wouldn't. If he could gain Yasmine's trust, he'd be able to work the truth out of her...or her computer hard drive.

Sure, he might have been able to gain the same information by breaking into her apartment, but he'd never have gotten access to Yasmine herself that way.

"Well," Alex said, fairly sure Drew didn't know anything. "I think I'm heading out of here. See you tomorrow, man."

"Sure, see you." Drew started humming jingle bells as he wheeled his chair back to his own cubicle.

Alex straightened the papers on his desk, powered down his computer, then stood and pushed in his chair. This damn cubicle was a reminder of everything he'd lost, and how he had nothing left to lose.

If he had nothing left to lose, then screw it. He'd do whatever it took to find out the truth about Yasmine.

2

"WHAT THE HELL is the matter with me?" Yasmine asked.

Cassandra Holbrook looked at Yasmine as though she'd lost her mind, then turned her attention back to sorting through the sale table in the Nordstrom accessories department. She unearthed a pink leather handbag and held it up to admire. "You're insane?"

"Possibly."

Only a day had passed since Kyle had asked Yasmine to the office party, and in the ensuing twenty-four hours she'd become obsessed with the idea. She'd done her usual ogling during work hours, but the staring had been accompanied by fantasies that had a very real possibility of happening. For the first time in a long while, she felt truly excited, exhilarated and jittery like a teenager looking forward to her first date. Now she wanted to find a gift for him, something to give him just for the sake of propriety, and then maybe something a little sexier to give him if all went the way she hoped it would.

Cass found a vanity mirror inside the pink handbag and checked her flawless makeup in it, then fluffed her wavy chestnut-brown hair before continuing to explore the bag's inner compartments.

Holiday shoppers milled about the downtown store, and a man wearing a lavender sweater edged Yasmine out of the way to grab a pair of discounted earmuffs. She elbowed herself back to her spot across from Cass and kept scanning the pile of merchandise for the perfect gift.

Yasmine had dialed her best friend's number on her way out of the office this afternoon and begged for some help picking out a gift for the hot guy she barely knew. Cass, as always, hadn't failed her. Never in her life had she missed an opportunity to shop.

"Why are you all of a sudden worried about your insanity?" asked Cassandra.

"This guy I'm buying the gift for? I think I've got a thing for him. And I'm pretty sure he won't want a pink handbag."

"Having the hots for him is a problem because...?"

"For one, he works with me, but more important, he's a total pretty boy."

"I'll never understand your aversion to beautiful men."

"I don't want a guy who's obsessed with appearances. And this guy has actual highlights. Like, the kind from the salon."

"So? Lots of men are getting color these days. I think it's sexy."

"Pretty soon men are going to be getting bikini waxes. That is *not* sexy."

"What planet have you been living on?"

Yasmine gaped at Cass. "Don't tell me men are becoming that obsessed with their appearances."

Lavender-sweater guy gave her a withering look, and she rolled her eyes at him.

"Honey, I hate to be the one to break it to you, but my last boyfriend recommended the woman who does my waxes now."

"Then why didn't he get the hair on his ass waxed off?" One of the many unwelcome tidbits of her love life Cass had foisted on Yasmine.

Cass shuddered. "Beats me. He brought a whole new meaning to the phrase 'love handles.'"

Yasmine grabbed a high-tech-looking no-spill coffee mug and decided it was possibly the most boring gift on earth. Clearly, she wasn't going to find the ideal present for Kyle here at the clearance table.

"I want a guy I won't have to compete with for time in front of the bathroom mirror."

"Maybe this new guy is just naturally beautiful. Then you've got the best of both worlds."

Yasmine bit her lip. "He does look kind of like a surfer. I guess it's possible he achieved natural highlights and a perfect tan in the great outdoors."

"See, you've just spent so many years around all those computer geeks in your office, you don't recognize a genuinely outdoorsy guy when you see one."

"Speaking of guys I work with, there's one I think you should go out with," Yasmine said, knowing there'd never be a perfect time to broach the subject of a blind date with Cass.

She stared across the sale table at Yasmine in abject horror. "You. Did not. Just suggest. A blind date."

"Yes. I did."

"Forget it!"

Admittedly, Cass had experienced some of the worst blind-date luck on the planet, and she seemed much happier without a guy in her life than she did with one. "This guy is different. He's smart, funny, nice, cute—"

"I don't do computer geeks, nerds or any other sort of New Economy professionals."

"So, what? You're eliminating ninety percent of the men in the Bay Area? Restricting yourself to impoverished teachers, janitors and the homeless?"

"I'm just being efficient, that's all. I know what I want, and I'm not going to waste my time on the losers who don't meet my criteria."

"You've been getting awfully picky lately," Yasmine blurted before she could catch herself. She'd danced around the subject of Cass's recent rejection of the dating scene, afraid of entering territory her friend didn't want to broach.

"In case you haven't noticed, I'm not getting any younger, and I've learned by now what I like and don't like. I know I've been telling people for the past decade or so that I'm twenty-nine, but—"

"You're not twenty-nine?" Yasmine tried her best to look genuinely shocked, but judging by Cass's expression, she'd failed.

"I'm actually thirty-nine, smart-ass."

"Well, you look amazingly young for your age."

"Thanks."

"I mean, in college, you really did blend in. You looked just as young as the rest of us."

Cass shrugged. "I worked at it. Dressed young, talked young, dated younger men. I guess it's become kind of a habit by now."

Yasmine resisted asking what seemed an obvious question—why bother to hide her age all this time? She knew Cass had her insecurities, but overall, she was one of the most confident women Yasmine knew.

"Do you think your friends will like you less if they think you're over thirty?"

"Well, sure. If I tell everyone now, they'll know I've been lying all this time."

"You don't have to lie to the next guy you date."

"Of course I do. That's the thing about lying—once you start, you've got to keep doing it."

Yasmine sighed. "If a guy is really worth your time, he won't care about your age."

"I care about my age. And that's what ultimately matters. I don't want to be over the hill."

"You're not even at the top of the hill yet. Besides, my work buddy wouldn't care at all about your age. He's probably in his mid to late thirties."

Cass liked to talk a good game about how she wasn't embarrassed of her past as a stripper, but it never quite rang true to Yasmine. She had a feeling this age thing was connected somehow.

"I'm going to pretend you never mentioned this whole blind-date idea to me. Let's get back to the far more interesting subject of you hooking up with the office hottie."

Yasmine decided the best approach wasn't to push any further. Drew's only hope with Cass would be if Yasmine could arrange for them to "accidentally" meet, but she'd have to bide her time now, wait for the right opportunity.

"Okay, okay," she said. "Yes, he's a hottie, But that doesn't change the fact that he's an office mate. What happens if we do hook up?"

"I dated the mailroom guy once for a few months."

"And I clearly remember you ducking into elevators

and broom closets to avoid him for months after the breakup."

"Oh, right. Well, then he moved to a new job, so no more ducking and dodging. And once I dated that guy from the public relations department."

"The spank-me guy—I remember him. How do you work with a guy after you've spanked him and asked him, 'Who's your mama?'"

Cass shrugged. "We only saw each other in passing after we broke up, and pretty soon he left the company, too. Nobody stays at the same job that long these days."

Yasmine examined a nearby rack of leather gloves, wallets and key fobs. Lousy gifts, all.

"Well, maybe everyone is moving to new jobs to escape old lovers. Maybe sleeping with him would make him leave the company, and then I could focus on my work again."

Or maybe she should just do what she secretly longed to do and declare her naughty intentions through her gift. She could give him some sensual massage oils or a cute pair of boxers or some toy handcuffs. Or a super-size box of condoms.

Too bad she'd learned the hard way that to get by in life, she had to control her rebellious impulses, no matter how tempting they might be.

She was in control now. Cursed to walk the straight and narrow path. Secure that her life would be boring but free from controversy for as long as she could help it.

A year in juvie prison would do that to a girl.

"Did I mention he asked me to be his date for the office Christmas party?"

Cass's jaw dropped. "And you said yes, I hope."

"Of course. But what if I can't stop staring at him or something?"

"Sounds like you just need to get laid."

"Maybe," Yasmine said, moving to a display of gifts for men, the usual prefab boxes of useless stuff no guy would ever buy for himself. She eyed a golf-themed desk set. "What are the chances he plays golf?"

"Sexual frustration can cloud good judgment," Cass said, "both for gift giving and choosing your dates."

"Maybe I should buy him a paper bag to wear over his head so I can concentrate on work."

Cass shrugged. "Or some See's chocolates. Who doesn't love those?"

One thought of See's chocolates and Yasmine's mind was made up, if for no other reason than setting foot in the store meant getting a free sample. "Done."

They headed across the mall, and five minutes later they were standing in the horrendous line that snaked through the small, stark-white store and out into the mall. It took fifteen minutes to finally make it to the front of the line.

Yasmine requested a sample of her favorite food on earth, a See's raspberry cream. "Mmm," she moaned when she bit into it. "Chocolate-covered sex."

The clerk behind the counter gave Yasmine a put-upon look, and since the line behind her was growing impatient to buy their yearly gift boxes and get the hell out of the mall, she said, "I'll take a pound of these."

Cass smiled. "You're buying him a whole pound of nothing but chocolate-covered sex?"

"It's a litmus test. If he gets what a great gift it is, then I take it as a sign he might be good in bed."

Her eyes lit up. "I should start doing that with all my dates."

And if all signs pointed to yes, then what? Did Yasmine sleep with the office hunk and risk ruining her long streak of good behavior?

She paid for her box of chocolates and headed out of the crowded store with Cass. "This is kind of a chintzy gift, though. Maybe I need a little something that declares my intentions subtly but clearly to go with it."

"Right. Something that could be interpreted as completely innocent or down and dirty, depending on your mind-set."

"What, like a jar of Vaseline?" Yasmine joked.

"Ew. On second thought, guys are kind of dense. Maybe you need to be loud and clear about your intentions. Maybe throw in a cute sex toy, and he'll get the hint."

"A nice big dildo?"

"Would you be serious for five seconds? I know a little sex shop a few blocks from here. How about a pair of furry handcuffs?"

Yasmine smiled. A quivery feeling was growing in her belly. It was the wild streak, rearing its stubborn head. And just this one time, she wanted to take out her long-ignored pet and play with it instead of keeping it hidden in the closet.

After so many years of being in control, Yasmine wasn't sure she could deny herself one hot, adventurous night of rebellion.

CASS HOLBROOK had never thought of herself as being destined for a corner office with a view, but over the years somehow, without her having completely realized it until now, she'd become respectable. She'd learned how to command attention without taking off her clothes.

So as she and Yasmine approached the mall Santa, on their way to the car, Cass was a little shocked to realize she hadn't done one of her infamous Santa stunts in years. She stopped a few feet from the velvet ropes that formed a line for waiting kids, and Yasmine turned, wearing a puzzled expression.

"What's wrong?"

"Have you told Santa what you want for Christmas?"

She was looking at Cass as if she'd lost it now. "Um, *no*."

"Then how do you expect to get what you want?"

"Have you been smoking something?"

"Don't you remember in college how we used to stand in line to sit on Santa's lap and tell him our naughty Christmas lists?"

Yasmine looked from Cass to the large man clad in red, and back again. "We were in college, and we were stupid."

Cass headed for the back of the line, which was only about ten kids deep. "So maybe we need to do more stupid things."

"Or not."

She waved Yasmine over, but she stood her ground.

"Come on, don't you want to see Santa's expression when I ask him for a—"

"Stop it! There are underaged people present," Yasmine said as she grabbed Cass's hand, and started tugging her away from the line.

"You've turned into such a prude," she said, letting herself be pulled toward the mall entrance.

Much as she loved Yasmine, Cass couldn't deny that her friend had taken her attempts to be a good girl to the extreme. The result was a sort of constipated life, a life wasted worrying too much about what was the right thing to do, a life that gave up interest to avoid risk. Cass had always seen herself as the answer to Yasmine's self-imposed uptightness, but now she realized she'd become just as uptight herself. Just as repressed. Not so much by shame over past misdeeds—although there were plenty—but by her focus on success. She'd been working so hard, she'd forgotten to have fun.

Now that Cass was coming out of the fog of her last dumping, she was beginning to notice some things about her life. Such as the fact that she was nearing the big four-oh and had managed to not acquire most of the traditional trappings of success: no husband, no kids, no house in the suburbs. Sure, she had a great career, a cute apartment and a fabulous wardrobe, but wasn't she supposed to want something more?

Where the hell was her ticking biological clock?

They reached the exit and Yasmine sighed as she held the door open. "What is going on with you?"

"Am I a freak of nature?"

"I thought that was a long-established fact," she said, but her smile softened the statement.

They walked out into the bustling sidewalk traffic outside the downtown mall and headed west toward the little upscale sex shop where Yasmine was sure to find any and every sexy gift imaginable. At the corner they stopped to wait for the light to change.

"I mean, aren't women of a certain age supposed to, you know, start wanting to settle down and be normal and stuff?" Cass said.

"There's no such thing as normal, and you're way too young to be worried about settling down, anyway."

Cass felt a stab of guilt for ever having lied to her own best friend about her age, but it was a lie she'd told years ago, when they'd first met, and she'd never quite gotten up the nerve to tell the truth until today. Anyway, it was sweet of Yasmine to still put her in the young category, even if it wasn't true.

Still, Cass felt liberated by having told the truth. And honestly, she was a little surprised to realize she was fine with turning forty.

"I guess you're right," she said as they crossed the street.

A cold breeze blew between the tall buildings, and Cass wrapped her long red scarf a few times around her neck and buttoned her white wool coat. They picked up their pace, and in a matter of minutes were at the sex shop.

Inside, seventies dance tunes played over the speakers, and aisle after aisle of every sex toy, accessory and undergarment imaginable stood on display. Yasmine hesitated at the entrance. Cass grabbed Yasmine's hand and tugged her toward the vibrator section.

Cass picked up a large, nubby hot-pink one from the top shelf and weighed it in her hand. "Might not be the greatest gift for a guy, but I, for one, would love to find this baby in my stocking."

"I'm not buying you a sex toy for Christmas," Yasmine said.

"And that's the difference between you and me. I

would buy one for you," Cass said as seriously as if she were offering to donate a vital organ.

"That's touching."

"No, honey, that's vibrating." She clicked the on button, and the toy in her hand hummed to life.

At practically the same moment, a new song came on, and suddenly Donna Summer was singing about her last dance of the night. Cass adored Donna Summer. In fact, it was pretty much a rule that no matter the time or place, if any of her songs came on, Cass felt compelled to launch into a full-fledged lip sync and dance routine.

Yasmine cast a wary look in her direction and started edging away toward the lingerie section. "You're not going to—"

Too late. "To-*night*," Cass belted out in time with the song, the vibrator held to her mouth like a microphone. Screw lip syncing. She knew this one by heart, so she could sing along for real.

She shimmied her hips to the music, dancing down the aisle, singing, the star of her own impromptu concert. This was the kind of craziness that had been missing from her life lately. This was what she needed to reclaim. It felt good…and right…and utterly silly.

Across the store from her now, Yasmine was trying hard to pretend they weren't together, but deep down, Cass knew Yasmine was loving every minute of it. The laughter she was struggling with told the real story. In a different life, without that old shadow of her year in juvenile detention hanging over her, she might have been the one belting out Donna Summer tunes into a dildo right now, and that was one of the things Cass loved about her. Yasmine had the heart of a wild child, even if she was living the life of an old lady.

Around Cass, other customers were taking notice. How could they not? Some smiled, some pretended she wasn't there, and some bee-bopped a little themselves as they shopped. The clerk who was working the store knew Cass and therefore understood her performance wasn't cause to call the cops.

As the song wound down and her routine came to an end, Cass replaced the vibrator on the shelf and went on shopping as if nothing out of the ordinary had taken place. Really, nothing had. She'd just gotten in touch with her true self, the side of her personality she loved most.

Yasmine was still across the store inspecting a rack of S & M apparel. But Cass was by herself and happy.

Happy, damn it. So what if she was happy? Could that ever really be a bad thing? So what if her boyfriend had dumped her and she'd had to pretend to not care about it?

She had her vibrator, her friends, her yearly trips to Cancun and her job, which she adored. Maybe there wasn't even room in her life for a serious relationship, and maybe…maybe she needed to stop feeling guilty about that.

Maybe she needed to accept, finally, at the age of almost-forty, that she was happy in every sense of the word.

ALEX FELT LIKE losing his lunch. For months he'd been preparing for this night, and he couldn't let a case of nerves blow his chance to gain Yasmine's trust.

He sat on the couch with his laptop and stared at his notes on Yasmine's case, the details of which had become as familiar to him as if they were events from his own life. But he needed to review them again to help himself remember why he was doing what he was doing. He had to keep his focus on her criminal record and off her more alluring attributes.

At the age of sixteen, going by the cybername Digital Diva, she'd broken into military computer databases and gotten caught, resulting in a one-year sentence in a juvenile detention center and a two-thousand-dollar fine.

For several years after her release, her Internet activities were under close watch by the FBI, but as she proved herself reformed, they'd backed off. As far as Alex could tell, she'd walked the straight and narrow path her entire adult life.

And while she'd stayed clean technically, during her senior year in college, she'd been targeted by the FBI as a possible member of a hacking ring known as The Underground that was suspected of being based at her university campus.

Alex had headed up the investigation of the group's illegal Internet activities, which had started out as petty vandalism but had escalated to more serious system intrusion jobs over a two-year period.

He'd never found any solid evidence that Yasmine was involved, but several of his colleagues, including his partner, Ty, had been sure she was a suspect to watch, and so he'd kept her on his radar.

Just as he'd thought he was making headway in the case, all of his files had been stolen, the FBI network had been hacked into and disabled and messages had been sent to all the top FBI authorities saying, "Down with the feds. Stop sending your hounds to sniff us out."

With his case against the hacker ring gone and head-quarters in a huff, Alex had been the whipping boy. And when one of his co-workers reported comments he'd made about finding Yasmine attractive, his integrity had been called into question. He'd been accused of being lax in his investigation because of his attraction to her, and in the cloudy uncertainty of hindsight, he often feared the accusation could be true.

In the fallout, he couldn't stop thinking about Yasmine, couldn't stop wondering if he'd been right or wrong and couldn't resist putting himself in a position to investigate her up close and personal.

The case was basically cold now—for him, anyway, since he didn't have access to FBI files anymore. But his investigator's instincts told him he'd missed something big, and he couldn't go about his normal life in peace until he knew for sure what it was he'd missed. The case haunted him, or perhaps more accurately, Yasmine haunted him.

Now what? He glanced at the clock in the corner of his computer screen. Still fifteen minutes before she was due to arrive at his house. He was keyed up about his first real chance to get close to her, to possibly gain her confidence. The only complication was his all-too-real attraction to her.

He needed to keep his mind off her physical beauty and focused on the fact that she potentially had the moral conscience of a reptile. She'd cost the government thousands of dollars with her juvenile crimes alone, and she'd never shown the slightest remorse for her actions.

He scrolled down the page of notes to a photo of her imbedded in the document. Yasmine, at seventeen, newly released from the detention center, caught on film by a local journalist. Her story had been plastered all over the news, mainly because she was young, brilliant, female and beautiful, as opposed to the typical gawky male hackers the public expected.

But one glance at her wide mouth, her soulful eyes, her satin skin, and his groin stirred. He was in a world of trouble if that's the amount of self-control he could muster for her. An image of her strutting around the office in slim-fitting pants came to mind, and he got a full-on erection.

Maybe he needed to go into the bathroom and take care of himself before she arrived, make sure his self-control was intact for his first evening with her.

But then the doorbell rang. Alex scrambled to save and close his document, then shut the laptop and went to the door. A glance through the window confirmed that it was Yasmine.

He adjusted himself in his pants, willed the woody to disappear—no luck there—and opened the door.

He'd dressed earlier in his best black suit and tie, but had been surprised to discover that his jacket had gotten a little too tight from his recent haunting of the gym. So he'd been forced to settle for a black vest instead. In the land that invented California casual, he was pretty sure no one would give a damn.

Yasmine surveyed his appearance and smiled. He hoped like hell she hadn't spotted the erection. His life had turned into a bad sitcom.

"Hey," she said. "Sorry I'm a little early. I had good traffic karma."

"Hey, yourself. You look great." His gaze dropped

straight to her cleavage. She wore a crimson velvet dress that dipped in a low vee at her chest, exposing the lush upper halves of her breasts, surprisingly full for her small frame. Yeah, he was being crude by staring.

He surveyed the rest of her, from her narrow waist to her long, firm legs exposed below her knee-length skirt, then lower to her feet adorned by a pair of do-me high heels. When he met her gaze again, she looked amused rather than annoyed.

"Thanks," she said. "Are you ready?"

Was he? If he could establish, at the very least, a friendship with Yasmine, eventually he could find out what he needed to know. But his body ached for a hell of a lot more than friendship.

"Yeah." He took off out the door with her.

Outside, the night had grown cool, and the sounds of the Inner Sunset neighborhood where he'd lived for the past five years filled the air with a cacophonic music he'd learned to love. He'd moved to San Francisco from Virginia for his first FBI assignment, and now he never wanted to leave.

He crammed himself into the passenger seat of her red Volkswagen Cabriolet, and when she got in on the driver's side, she looked at his knees pressed against the dashboard and laughed.

"Guess my ride wasn't made for tall people."

He tried to adjust his legs but couldn't. "Most cars aren't."

"You can move the seat back with the levers on the side."

A minute later he had enough leg room and had adjusted the seat until he was comfortable, or at least as much as he could be in Yasmine's presence. She drove like a woman with a serious case of road rage, and he had to bite his tongue to keep from insisting she pull over and let him take the wheel.

"You're being awfully quiet," she said, glancing at him at the same time she was tailgating a Toyota.

"You're scaring me," he said, grinning. "Anyone ever tell you that you drive like a lunatic?"

She laughed. "Um, yeah. I'll try to restrain myself."

So would he.

"So are you spending the holidays with your family?" she asked.

"Actually, no. My brother and parents rented a place in Hawaii, but I couldn't get the time off to join them, since I'm the new guy in the office."

She seemed about to say something, but didn't.

"How about you?" he asked.

"My parents are the only family I have around here, and they took off on a trip last week, so I guess I'm spending the weekend solo."

Alex's body tensed slightly. Could he take advantage of this opportunity? He wouldn't be acting exactly in the spirit of the season if he did whatever it took to find out the truth about Yasmine. His guilty conscience nagged him for all of a few seconds before he decided, screw it—if she was guilty, the time of year didn't matter.

If tonight went the way he hoped it would, he'd have her confessing all the details of her life—criminal and otherwise—by the end of the weekend.

"So if you're all alone, and I'm all alone…"

"Doesn't seem right, does it?"

"We could keep each other company—maybe go out for a movie and Chinese food?" And maybe, if he played his cards right, something more.

3

"SURE, WE COULD HANG OUT tomorrow. That sounds like fun," Yasmine said, and Alex heaved a silent sigh of relief.

One hurdle crossed, countless more to go.

Fifteen harrowing minutes later, they'd arrived miraculously unscathed at the downtown hotel where the party was being held. Alex loosened his death grip on the door handle and tossed Yasmine a look as the valet parking attendants came to open their doors.

"What?" she said as she checked her hair in the rearview mirror, Miss Innocent all of a sudden.

"I'm driving us home."

She shrugged. "Okay, if you know how to drive a stick."

"I know how to do all kinds of things," he heard himself say. It was unplanned, stupid and tacky, but instead of slapping him, she looked him up and down.

"I'm looking forward to a demonstration," she said, a smile playing on her lips, a note of flirtation in her tone, right before she got out of the car.

He walked with her through the lobby to the event room where the party was already well under way. Yasmine turned to him and smiled as they stood inside the entrance. "Looks like we'll be the main topic for office gossip tonight."

People he recognized and others he didn't turned to stare at them.

Alex shrugged. "Glad to add a little interest to the evening."

Christmas Eve was tomorrow and they had Monday off, so no one was scheduled to return to work until Tuesday. Not a chance anyone would forget in that short time, but whatever. He didn't exactly give a damn.

Not giving a damn meant he could endure the winks and nudges of his male office mates, most of whom considered Yasmine to be the catch of all catches.

Being a programming genius and having a reputation as a former hacker only added to her mystique. In their eyes, bagging her would make him a god among programmers.

Yasmine slipped her hand into his and led him across the room to an empty table. "Hope you don't mind if we sit alone," she said.

"Want a drink?"

She nodded. "Champagne would be great."

Alex made his way through the crowd to the bar, then returned to the table with the drinks and sat down next to her.

Yasmine took a sip of champagne, then said, "Tell me about yourself. How long have you been programming?"

"Too long. Probably since before you were out of diapers."

She rolled her eyes. "Please. We're the same age, aren't we? How old are you?"

At thirty-five, he was nine years older than her, but he didn't see any reason to point that out. "Thirty-one."

That's how old Kyle Kramer was, anyway.

"Oh. You *are* an older man then," she said, grinning.

He raised his eyebrows. "Do I have to ask how old you are?"

But he knew. She was twenty-six as of July 15.

"I'm old enough," she said, leaving the unspoken question "For what?" hanging in the air.

"I'll bet." Old enough to know better, but that had never stopped her from breaking the rules before. Alex found himself hoping she'd continue to be wild for at least one more night.

"Mind if we sit here?"

Alex looked up to see Drew Everton, sans Santa hat, and a woman who must have been his date standing on the other side of the table.

Much as Alex wanted to be alone with Yasmine, he couldn't think of any polite reason to say no. "Sure, have a seat," he said instead.

"Kyle, Yasmine, this is my friend Hannah Filarski," Drew said as he pulled out a chair for her.

She sat down and beamed across the table at them. "Hi!" she said a little too loudly.

"Hi," Alex said. "Where did you and Drew meet?"

He caught the wince Drew gave at that question as he sat down next to Hannah.

"We met through an online dating service. Drew's my twentieth match so far."

"Wow, that's a lot of dating," Yasmine said.

"I'm on a mission to find Mr. Right before the end of the year." She glanced at her watch. "And I have exactly eight days, four hours and twenty-two minutes to find him."

"She's joking," Drew said, then forced a laugh.

"No, I'm not." Her wide smile took on a brittle quality. "I had my cards read at the beginning of the year, and they said I'd definitely find my one true love this year."

Yasmine glanced at Alex, then quickly looked away, amusement twinkling in her eyes. "Maybe that just meant you'd *meet* him this year. But you might not realize he's the one until months or years later."

This apparently was not the answer Hannah was looking for. "No, I definitely have to know it's him right away. Biological clock and all," she said, as if Yasmine, at twenty-six, understood such things.

Alex, oddly enough, was beginning to understand the ticking of the clock. Not that he felt as if his time would run out at midnight on the thirty-first, but he did find himself wondering when and if he'd ever have the chance to test that all the equipment was working properly.

And Yasmine's words kept echoing in his head. *You might not realize he's the one until months or years later.* A nagging voice in his head wanted to know why Yasmine had lingered in his mind all these years. Why, of all the cases he'd worked on, of all the women he'd known, was she the one he couldn't forget?

Was it possible that only now, nine years after she'd first laid eyes on him from across the witness stand, Yasmine might realize he was The One?

And where the hell had that idea come from? He knew whatever he started with her would be doomed, so there was no point in imagining a future. Women generally didn't fall for the men who'd sent them to prison.

He'd managed to tune out the conversation that had been happening at the table. He started paying attention and found Drew still looking uncomfortable, and Hannah discussing how she'd eliminated all her former matches through a careful and insane process of critiquing their shoes.

"So, let me get this straight," Yasmine said. "You can sum up a guy by the shoes he chooses to wear on a first date?"

"Absolutely," Hannah said.

"But what if your dream guy is on his way to the car to pick you up for your first date, wearing the right shoes, and he steps in a pile of dog crap, then goes back in and changes into the wrong pair of shoes?" Drew asked.

Hannah seemed caught off guard by the question, but after a few awkward moments she recovered and answered, "If he's Mr. Right, then the second pair of shoes he chooses will also be the right shoes."

Alex was beginning to wish Hannah would go off in search of a pile of dog crap instead of staying here to inflict any more of this conversation on him.

"So you must have already sized Drew up based on his footwear," Yasmine said. "How does he fare by your shoe standards?"

"I never do the analysis while *on* the date," Hannah said.

Of course not. That would be crazy.

"So when do you do it?"

"I simply take detailed mental notes during the date, and then afterward I write it all out and decide what his shoe choices mean for my destiny."

"I personally think it's what's in the shoe that counts. I could never love a guy with bad feet," Yasmine said, her tone teasing as she cast a glance down at Alex's Bruno Magli's.

"Ew, I hate feet! They're just so gross." This, from Hannah of the shoe-analysis method of dating.

"I think they're sexy," Yasmine said, then sipped her champagne. "Our company recently designed an interactive software program for foot fetishists."

Hannah didn't seem to know what to say to that. "So…you guys make sex software? What, exactly, does that mean?"

"Have you ever heard of the game Virtual Bimbo? It's our bestselling product."

"Virtual *Bimbo?*" Hannah looked horrified. "As a woman, don't you find that offensive?"

"I actually think it's hilarious. The game allows you to design your own bimbo, and then you take her out on the club scene and try to get her laid."

The look of horror grew.

"It's supposed to be funny," Drew added.

"You win the game if she scores with the hottest guy in the club," Yasmine said, seeming to enjoy Hannah's discomfort, "and you lose if she has to go home with the weenie guy. The final video sequence shows her having sweaty, multiple-orgasm sex if it's the hot guy, or boring rabbit sex with the weenie guy."

"Oh my God, that's awful."

Drew made a throat-clearing sound and said, "So, Kyle, what did you do before you came to VirtualActive?"

Alex had rehearsed his answer a hundred times in his head, until he could spout it as if it were the truth. And it really wasn't that far from the truth. "I worked as a programmer in Virginia for a while, then got burned out on that, came to California and started a survival training business."

"Survival training," Yasmine said. "You mean like living in the wild and killing your own food?"

"Those are a few of the skills I taught." In truth, he'd spent summers in college teaching survival training in the mountains of Virginia, so it was a natural choice for his fake previous career.

"So that's where you got the big muscles and the tan," she said. "Certainly not from sitting at a computer all day."

"Please don't tell me you killed actual animals," Hannah said, the color gone from her cheeks.

"We tried hunting teddy bears, but no one could bring themselves to eat the polyester stuffing."

He didn't see any point in getting into the whole issue of killing one's food to eat. It wasn't something he'd ever enjoyed doing—matter of fact, he'd hated it—but it was an essential element of survival in the wild.

Under the table, Yasmine's foot nudged his, and she was trying hard not to smile.

Hannah pushed herself away from the table and stood. "I can't sit here with someone who kills animals for sport."

Drew looked at her without making a move to stand as well. "Um…would you like a ride home?"

"I'll take a cab!" she said and walked away.

Drew sighed as he looked from Alex to Yasmine. "And that is the official end of my adventures in online dating."

"So I guess her dream guy's shoes would be made of cruelty-free materials," Yasmine said.

"Sorry, man, I didn't mean to open a can of worms," Alex said.

"I'm sorry, too, but she had to go," Yasmine said. "You can do a hundred times better than her."

Drew made a face and shrugged, then downed his drink. "I knew it was a doomed date when she made a big fuss over my driving a car with a gas-powered engine. Apparently, she prefers guys who use electric."

"I told you, I've already got the perfect woman for you. I just need to figure out a way to hook you up," Yasmine said.

"Well, whatever. I think I'm going to grab some chow over there at the buffet," Drew said as he stood up from the table.

Across the room, the band transitioned from playing holiday music Alex had been ignoring, to an up-tempo dance number, and people began to fill the dance floor. He craned his head to watch, unable to resist the spectacle of a bunch of techno-geeks dancing without rhythm.

"Want to dance?" Yasmine said.

"Um…" He didn't especially, but he loved the idea of watching her dance. "Sure."

A few seconds later that's exactly what he was doing, and Yasmine's moves were even hotter than he'd imagined. Mesmerized by the sway of her hips, he forgot about everyone else in the room.

They danced through one song, then another and another. Finally a slow song came on, and they moved close together.

Her hands slid up his chest, around his neck. Their first real physical contact. Her body pressed against him, moving to the slow beat of the music, coaxing him into an intimate dance with a promise of something more.

Where their bodies met, he burned.

He wanted her, no getting around it, no ignoring it for a second; his body wouldn't let him. And as he grew hard against her, she couldn't help but know it too.

Then she did something unexpected. She pressed her abdomen more firmly against him, against his erection, stoking his desire. Her gaze sparked with daring.

"I've got a thing for you, you know," she said into his ear.

"You do?"

"And it has nothing to do with your feet."

"I've got good feet, just so you know."

She smiled. "I've been having trouble concentrating at work."

"Because of me?"

She nodded, her eyes locked on his.

"I'd hate to affect your job performance."

"Then I think we need to come up with a fix for this."

The last shred of Alex's will to resist disappeared. Whatever fix she proposed, he was all over it.

What the hell. Didn't he deserve one night without self-control? He wanted Yasmine, she wanted him— what was the harm in giving in to their urges? If anything, it would help him get closer to her, right?

Right.

The music changed to an Elvis rendition of "White Christmas." Alex took Yasmine's hand and led her off the dance floor.

Who needed mistletoe and chestnuts roasting on an open fire? They'd started a fire of their own, and it was time to put it out.

As they passed a huge, twinkling Christmas tree at

the edge of the dance floor, she tugged him behind it and pinned him against the wall, where they were concealed from the crowd. Her hand grazed his thigh, then traveled across his pelvis, barely missing his cock. A smile played on her lips, and he knew she was teasing him.

"Am I being too forward?" she asked.

"I like a woman who knows what she wants."

"So you're getting my message loud and clear?"

"I think so," he whispered as he traced his finger along the neckline of her dress, brushing the soft flesh of her breast as he did so.

"Let me spell it out for you," she whispered. "I want you to take me home and have hot, nasty sex with me all night long."

He went from half-mast to full in an instant. This didn't feel like an investigation. It just felt right. He couldn't think of anything he wanted more than Yasmine naked in his bed.

"Right now?"

"Right now."

"What about dinner? Aren't you hungry?"

"Not for food, but we can pick up carryout on the way home."

Alex didn't need any further invitation.

He took her by the waist and guided her out from behind the Christmas tree. Through the crowd, out the door, across the hotel lobby, to the parking lot—he didn't stop until they were at the valet parking stand.

"You think everyone will forget about our having shown up here together by Tuesday?" she asked as they waited for her car.

"Not a chance."

"You think we'll inspire a new sex game idea? Maybe a holiday-themed one—Christmas Party Hookup?"

Alex laughed. "If that's the title of our next software release, we'll know where the idea came from."

"I guess a little gossip's not so bad. They'll have something more interesting to talk about than the latest gadgets they got for Christmas."

"You don't care what people think?"

"It doesn't make any difference if I care. People will think what they want to think."

That was probably the attitude that helped her remain a criminal without remorse.

For a moment Alex came to his senses and felt the urge to stop this speeding train while he still had the chance. But he glanced over at Yasmine, her face lit by the glow of the hotel lights, and the doubt disappeared. He'd wanted her for years, now he could get rid of all that wanting.

Yasmine had exposed to him his biggest weakness, and it was her.

4

YASMINE HAD SPENT way too many years controlling her rebellious impulses. But she'd learned her lesson as a teenager—rebellion can have consequences. Severe consequences.

She followed Kyle up the stairs to his apartment and tried to ignore the whirl of excitement growing in her belly. What she should do was eat some Kung Pao Chicken, kiss Kyle good-night, and go home. Forget this whole crazy sex idea. She knew better by now than to follow her wild impulses, because they'd only ever led her into serious trouble.

Hacking had started out as simply an interesting challenge. She'd been a typical teenager—bored, angry and sick of her parents—only, with a gift for invading computer systems. Then hacking had grown into an act of defiance when she'd realized how much power she wielded on the Internet, and how much it would piss off her oblivious parents if they found out what she'd been up to.

Of course, they found out right before the whole world did, and they'd been furious. For once, she'd had their undivided attention.

Teen Girl Hacks Government Computers had been

one of the many headlines splashed across newspapers. Her parents had thought granting the press permission to use her photo would teach her a lesson, but all the exposure had really accomplished was to create a weird cult of celebrity around her and the case.

In the months before her trial, she'd had to close her e-mail account because of all the whacked messages she'd received from guys who thought she was the hottest thing since Internet porn.

The two-year period of her prosecution and imprisonment was the worst of her life. She'd prided herself on learning a lesson from the ordeal, and she'd vowed not to cross paths with the law again.

But some little part of her, some barely controllable impulse, ached to go wild again. She didn't have to break the law. In fact, she saw now that maybe she'd gone a little too far in the opposite direction, trading in an interesting life for the confines of a law-abiding one.

She'd become too good at avoiding trouble.

She could back out now, while Kyle was unlocking his front door.

And then what?

She'd spend the rest of her life—or at least the rest of the long, lonely weekend—regretting her caution. This was a night that begged for action.

Kyle would be her Christmas gift to herself. She'd been working hard to stay under control, depriving herself, and now she deserved a night of wild, guilt-free sex.

Didn't she? She could even call it career development, since she'd gotten so far out of touch with her sensual that she'd started feeling like a fraud in the sex software business.

He stepped aside so she could enter the apartment, and once they were both in, he switched on a lamp.

"Are you sure about this?" she asked halfheartedly, her self-control in its death throes.

"You want to stop?" he asked, taking a step closer to her and brushing a strand of hair away from her cheek.

"Hell, no."

She ached, she burned, she nearly hummed with the anticipation of finally getting Kyle up against her, inside her, all over her for a night.

Yasmine shrugged off her velvet dress coat and let it fall to the floor, as Kyle dropped their Chinese takeout on a nearby table and turned to her. He removed his tie, then his vest, letting both fall near their feet.

He pulled her to him and gave her what was possibly the hottest kiss she'd ever had. His tongue danced with hers while his hands explored her, down her sides, over her butt. He lifted up her dress and cupped her black-lace-encased backside, handling her possessively, as if staking a claim to his territory.

Then he lifted her up and pinned her against the door, his hips pressed between her legs, pushing her dress up around her waist. Yasmine squirmed, wanting him even closer.

"Do you have protection?" she asked when they finally broke their kiss.

"In the bathroom." But he made no move to end their embrace.

Instead, his hands traveled up her rib cage to cup her breasts. She'd noticed him admiring them earlier, as most men did, and she'd been plagued by images of Alex kissing her breasts ever since.

His fingertips teased her nipples, coaxing them into a rock-hard state. "You're beautiful," he murmured.

"So are you."

His gaze took on a hint of amusement. "Oh, yeah?"

Then he kissed her again. He carried her down the hallway to a bedroom, where he tossed her on the bed.

"I'll be right back," he said, and disappeared into the bathroom.

Yasmine glanced down at her rumpled state and sighed. Clothes were only going to get in the way, so she got up and hurriedly undressed down to her matching bra and panties, her thigh-high stockings and heels. Then she climbed onto the bed again and arranged herself just so.

When Kyle returned, he stopped in his tracks, his gaze darkening as he took in her appearance. He closed the distance between them, dropped a box of condoms next to her, and stood at the edge of the bed as he stripped out of his clothes. Yasmine watched in appreciation as every inch of flesh she'd been spending too much time at work imagining was finally revealed to her in all its glory.

No Playboy bunny tattoo, thankfully.

Naked, he climbed on top of her and molded his body to hers. His erection pressed against her panties, creating a delicious pressure where she wanted it most.

Okay, so maybe doing it with a pretty-boy wasn't so bad. Maybe she needed to revisit her rules for guy selection, if having a guy as gorgeous as Kyle in her bed got her this hot.

His hair tickled her cheek as he bent to kiss her, and she wrapped her arms and legs around him, wanting all of him at once.

"You like it hot and nasty?" he whispered.

That's what she'd said at the party, after all. "Hot and nasty, slow and sweet—whatever the situation calls for."

He rolled them over so that she was on top, and she knew the situation tonight definitely called for the kind of sex where they'd both break a sweat. There was no other way, when she wanted him this badly, this urgently.

She took off her panties, and he freed her of the bra in one skilled flick of his wrist. Then she straddled his hips and pressed herself against him, testing her own will.

It wasn't very strong.

With her gaze locked on his, she edged her way down until she was between his legs and her breath caressed his cock. She licked the length of him, and air whooshed from his lungs. She took him all the way in her mouth, and his hands grasped the blanket beneath them as he strained toward her. She trailed her tongue up and down, then around, savoring the hot, hard feel of him, loving the power she held over his body.

Tickling his balls with her fingernails, she quickened her pace, then slowed again when she could feel him tensing more.

"Yasmine," he said, more a moan than a word. "Please."

She stopped. "Please what?"

"I want you," he whispered.

"Now?"

"Now."

She grabbed the box of condoms, removed one, then opened the packet with her teeth. When she took his erection in her hand, their gazes met again for a moment.

She slid the condom on him, taking her time, playing her fingers along the ridges of his cock, exploring new territory. He was big, really big. Deliciously big. Her fingers grazed his balls again, and his eyes fluttered shut as he expelled a sigh of pleasure.

He did have tan lines, at his waist and on his thighs, but the most obvious ones were on his forearms, at his wrists.

"You surf?" she asked, imagining how cold the water must be this time of year, certainly cold enough to warrant a full-body wet suit.

"Yeah. You?"

"Hell, no. I like to look at the ocean, not get in it."

He smiled. "It's not so bad once you're out there. Maybe I could give you lessons sometime."

"I've got a different kind of sport in mind for us."

His eyebrows quirked. "Something you need lessons for?"

"I don't think I do. I've had some practice," she said, straddling him again, then rocking her hips, rubbing her slick, wet center against his cock.

"Practice makes perfect." His gaze was locked on hers as he lifted her hips and buried himself deep inside her.

Yasmine expelled a pent-up breath as he stretched her, as the sweet burning of her body molding to him became the single thought on her mind.

She covered his hands with hers as he massaged her breasts, and she began rocking her hips in a steady rhythm, getting to know his moves as he got to know hers. Tossing her hair over one shoulder, it became a curtain over their hands, over her breast.

Men loved her hair, she knew, and she'd always kept it long because it made her different. Alex took a chunk of it and roped it around his hand, gently exploring the texture.

The thumb of his other hand dipped between her legs to massage her clit, and she forgot everything but that incredible building of pressure.

Her pace quickened more as his cock probed deeper and deeper inside her, as her body coiled tighter and tighter until she knew she was only moments from climax.

And he stopped. Stilled her hips with his hands, hovering half in and half out of her.

"Not so fast," he whispered, his own voice strained enough that she knew exactly the sort of self-control he possessed.

She leaned forward and licked his lower lip. "Finish what you've started."

"Sex is like waiting for the perfect wave," he said, then nipped her own lower lip gently with his teeth.

"I don't remember agreeing to any lessons tonight."

He flexed his cock inside her, creating a frenzy of sensation in her nether regions. "You've got to be patient," he said. "Wait it out, and the payoff could be a ride you'll never forget."

ALEX FELT HIS HANDS tremble at the effort of restraining himself. His desire for Yasmine was like a force of nature, a cresting wave he could do nothing to stop, but had only to jump on and ride to shore.

And yet, he wanted to savor this. There might never be another night with this woman who'd haunted him so deeply for so long. No more careening toward the shore too quickly.

He grasped her hips and tugged her forward, tugging still when she resisted. She fell forward and kissed him, working her tongue against his the same way she'd worked it against his cock. And, damn had she ever worked his cock. It had taken every ounce of his self-control not to come in her mouth.

He broke the kiss. "I want to taste you."

"You just did."

"I want to taste your pussy."

"Mmm, can't argue with that," she said, a smile playing on her damp lips.

She let him tug her hips forward then, until she was straddling his neck, holding onto the headboard for support, and he could flick out his tongue and taste her.

"Lower," he commanded. And then he was there, his mouth against her, his tongue inside her where she was hottest.

The sound of her moans spurred him on. He took her clit in his mouth and sucked gently until she was squirming and gasping, then he slipped two fingers inside her, three fingers, in and out, stretching her walls and giving her eager muscles something to contract against.

She was so close to coming, he could almost taste it—couldn't wait to taste it. With his middle finger, he found her G-spot and caressed her there, sending her crying out over the edge.

As she swayed her hips, dripping wet against him, in the final waves of her orgasm, he felt the trembling return. Urging him forward. He couldn't wait any longer to be inside her again.

Clasping her waist, he urged her down his torso until she was straddling his hips again. He positioned himself under her and held her still as he thrust inside. In that one thrust, all his pent-up desire, all the years of wanting her, started to find its release, and he could only hold on, savoring every sensation.

He loved the way her long hair created a peek-a-boo show with her breasts. The glimpse of her nipples, dark and erect, spurred him closer to orgasm, and the flat smooth expanse of her belly, ending in the small triangle of hair where their bodies met, sent him over the edge.

Pleasure coursed through him in waves, until he could only pull her close and catch his breath with his face nuzzled in her neck. They lay tangled together until their combined heat became uncomfortable and they broke apart to cool off.

Alex watched Yasmine, fascinated by the way pleasure softened her features. His own emotions on the heels of their lovemaking were...confused. He didn't want to think about the possible complications.

"You know, we've still got dinner to eat," he said after they'd lain in silence for a short while, finally hungry now that he'd had his temporary fill of Yasmine.

"Oh, right," she rolled over and stretched. "I am hungry now that you mention it."

They climbed out of bed, and Alex pulled an old William and Mary College shirt out of his dresser drawer, then tossed it to Yasmine. He watched as she tugged it on, admiring the curves of her body one more time before they were hidden by the baggy shirt. She found her panties on the floor and put those on, too, as he dressed himself in a pair of reindeer-print boxers and a black tee.

She smiled at his boxers. "Cute."

"Me or the reindeer?"

"Both. I like a man who can wear goofy underwear."

"All in the spirit of the season."

She followed him out of the bedroom and into the wide area that Alex used as his living area and office combined. He switched on a lamp. A wide, low cocktail table in front of the couch served as his dining room, and as he looked around the space, seeing it through Yasmine's eyes—the bachelor-pad sparseness, the unsightly stacks of bills and magazines, the cheesy San Francisco posters that served as wall art—he had a horrible realization.

He should never have brought her to his apartment. Somehow, in the frenzy of getting her alone and naked, he'd overlooked the fact that she could stumble on any number of items here that would make it glaringly, obviously clear he was not who he pretended to be. His mail, his magazines, his drug prescriptions, all announced his name was Alex DiCarlo, and photos in his albums showed him mostly as the short-haired, clean-cut FBI agent he used to be, not the long-haired surfer he'd become.

Damn it, he was a freaking idiot. Idiot, idiot, idiot.

Before she'd come to pick him up, he'd taken a quick glance around to make sure there was no incriminating evidence lying about, so he knew the living room was at least superficially safe. But he needed to make a closer inspection, and fast.

"Sorry this place is kind of a mess," he said.

"Don't worry about it." She started removing the cartons of food from the carryout bags and placing them on the cocktail table.

Making as though he was cleaning up, he grabbed the stacks of magazines and bills sitting on the end table and carried them to a closet, where he shoved them on the top shelf.

"I'll get some silverware," she said, heading for the kitchen.

"No, wait, I'll get it," he said a little too quickly. "I think I left dirty dishes on the counter."

She gave him an odd look. "Really, it's okay," she said, but lowered herself to the floor beside the table.

In the kitchen, he glanced around for more incriminating evidence. The answering machine blinked at him with a message waiting, so turned it off to avoid any disastrous "Hey, Alex" messages. A few pieces of mail lay on the counter near the phone. He grabbed them up and shoved them in a drawer beneath the phone book, then found the silverware.

"What would you like to drink?" he called into the living room. "I have beer, water, milk and OJ."

"Guess I'll take a beer, then."

He emerged from the kitchen carrying two Heinekens, plates, forks and serving spoons, then arranged it all on the cocktail table.

"I need to use the bathroom," he said. "I'll be right back. Go ahead and start without me."

Inside his small bathroom, he threw open the medicine cabinet and scooped out the labeled prescription medicine, then wrapped it all in a towel and stowed it in the back of the cabinet under the sink. After relieving himself and washing his hands, he went to the bedroom and gave it a quick survey for more evidence of his real identity.

For once, his lack of effort in making his apartment

a personal space seemed to be paying off. The only thing he needed to hide in his bedroom was an old photo of himself and his brother, which he stowed in a dresser drawer. Entering the hallway again, he bumped into Yasmine leaving the bathroom.

"Just needed to wash my hands," she said. "What are you doing?"

"Hiding some dirty laundry from you."

She grinned. "I've been in bachelor pads before. Socks on the floor are not going to shock me."

"I'd at least like your first impression to be something besides 'hopeless slob.'"

"Trust me, your first impression is safe," she said, glancing down at his crotch—or was it his reindeer boxers?

"What's that supposed to mean?" he said as he followed her down the short hallway.

She turned and slid her arms around his waist, peering up at him. "It means, when you give a girl the kind of ride you just gave me, she's not going to give a damn what your apartment looks like."

His cock, predictable as it was, stirred against her abdomen. At the same time, his stomach growled, and she glanced down at the sound.

"We'd better feed you so you'll have energy for later."

For later. A jolt of satisfaction shot through him to know that there'd be more, that this wasn't just a one-shot deal.

In the living room again, Alex grabbed two large pillows from the sofa and tossed them on the area rug as makeshift floor pillows. "Dining doesn't get any finer than this," he said as he motioned for her to sit.

She smiled. "I'm a simple girl. Great sex, good carry-out—it doesn't take a lot to make me happy."

They dug into the food and ate in silence for a few minutes. Alex hadn't realized just how hungry he was until he'd devoured most of his shrimp fried rice and looked up to see Yasmine staring at his work space on the other side of the room.

"Looks like you've got a whole business set up there," she said, and the food in his stomach turned to stone.

He did all his security business work from home, and if she looked closely enough, she'd be able to figure it out.

He shrugged. "I'm a computer geek—what can I say?"

"Bet my system's better than your system," she taunted.

"Did you build it yourself?"

"Yeah, you?"

He nodded. "Play your cards right and I might show you what's inside the CPU case, water-cooled system and all."

"We're verging on sounding like the world's biggest geeks, you know."

"Yeah." He grinned. "We should stop while we're still ahead."

She cast a curious glance at him. "What exactly are we doing here?"

"Eating fried rice and Kung Pao chicken?"

"I mean you and me. Are we going to pretend this never happened come Tuesday?"

"I know the whole sleeping-with-a-coworker thing can get awkward," he said, buying time until he could think of the best angle.

"Maybe we should establish some ground rules."

"Is this a one-night thing?" he asked, hoping like hell it wasn't. "Or do you see this happening again?"

She smiled and glanced down at his bare feet. "You do have nice feet," she said.

He slid his foot closer, then trailed his toes along her inner thigh until they made contact with her panties. He found her clit with his big toe and massaged, watching as her eyes fluttered shut.

"Mmm," she moaned, letting her fork clatter onto the plate.

"Are you avoiding my question?" he teased, pushing aside the narrow crotch of her panties and slipping his toe inside her.

"No…not avoiding…" She reached down and stilled his foot, then gently pushed it away, still holding it between her legs. "If you keep that up, we'll never finish dinner."

"Just reminding you of what you could be missing out on."

She stroked his wet toe with her fingertips. "Does that mean you want this to be more than a one-night thing?"

"I figure, I'm alone this weekend, you're alone—"

"We might as well keep each other company," she filled in.

Alex heaved a sigh of relief. "Exactly. I can understand the need for ground rules. Like, no talking about what happens this weekend with coworkers."

"Do we need to set some kind of time limit to keep things simple? Like, when the weekend is finished, so are we?"

It was a rule that worked to his advantage, giving him time to find out the truth about Yasmine, then extract himself from her life before any messy emotions got involved. So he had no idea why her suggestion felt like a punch to the gut. Had to be stupid male pride getting in the way.

"That sounds fair, but we could always reevaluate later."

"And no hard feelings after the fact. We go back to work, and we're friends. Deal?"

He extended his pinky finger, and she intertwined hers with his. "Deal," he said.

Then they shook on it.

5

ALEX FELT SOMETHING warm and soft against him. He shifted his weight toward the warmth and came in contact with solid flesh. He opened his eyes and saw the back of Yasmine's head, her dark hair spilling over the pillow.

Then the memories of last night came flooding in. Flesh against flesh, tangled limbs, hot kisses, even hotter sex. They'd kept going until his leg muscles trembled and his body was spent. Then they'd collapsed on the bed, in each other's arms, and slept the night away.

He yawned and stretched. From the window, light poured in, diffused by fog.

It was Christmas Eve, and morning fog was about as winter wonderland as San Francisco weather got.

This was normally one of Alex's favorite days of the year, but this year, the holiday promised to be memorably different if it played out the way he hoped. If he convinced Yasmine to let him spend the night—maybe the whole weekend—at her place….

Next to him, she stirred. Her leg moved against his, the satin skin of her thigh warming him, then she rolled onto her back and peered at him through half-lidded eyes. In the morning light, with her makeup gone and her hair a mess, she looked amazing.

"Hey," he said, his voice groggy from sleep.

He hated that he was so mesmerized by her, even after all these years. She had the power to make him lose his mind.

"Hey, yourself," she whispered, eyeing his bare chest. "Did we, um, do something last night?"

"You don't remember?"

Her straight face gave way to a smile. "Sorry, bad joke. Yes, I remember."

She traced his jaw with her fingers and then leaned forward and placed a kiss on his lips. "Last night was fun."

"Mmm-hmm. You have any big last-minute shopping plans today?"

"Actually, no plans at all other than hanging out with you."

This was his chance, but there was a risk of overplaying his hand. She wore a blissed-out expression, though, that told him now was the time, while the memories of their night together were still hot and vivid.

He slid his hand across her belly, a featherlight touch that caused her nipples to harden. Up her rib cage his hand went, then to her breasts where he traced her areolas with his fingertips.

"What do you say we spend the day in bed?"

She smiled and arched her back, stretching her arms over her head. "I'd say you've got filthy intentions toward me."

She draped her leg over his and rolled onto him, resting her chin on his chest.

"I might say the same thing about you."

She ground her hips against him, and he could feel the hot dampness between her legs on his thigh. Instantly he grew hard.

"I think I made my intentions pretty clear last night," she said.

"Are you always so bold?" he asked, though he was pretty sure he knew the answer—that she was much too bold for her own good.

And why that caused him a pang of concern, he couldn't say.

"Maybe. Are you always so good in bed?"

"With the right woman."

Though last night was not usual. He'd been on fire as he'd never been before. That's what happened, he supposed, when he spent a decade waiting and wanting a woman he knew he shouldn't have.

She was even better than he'd imagined.

But there were so many fantasies he'd entertained. So many ways he'd imagined taking her, pleasuring her, having her to do with as he pleased. He'd need the whole weekend to do those fantasies justice, no doubt, and he'd need just as much time to find the truth he was looking for.

"I guess it would be tacky to not even get out of bed on Christmas Eve," she said.

"I don't know. I mean, as long as we're together, it sort of goes along with the spirit of giving, right?"

"Actually, maybe we could take this back to my place. I've got a cat who needs to be fed."

Thank heaven for cats.

"Sounds good to me," he said, all casual and aloof, as though she hadn't just invited him to snoop around in her life.

Her hand was traveling down his chest, and by the time she made it to his erection, he'd forgotten what he'd been thinking about.

"There's no big hurry. The cat can wait a few hours, but I, on the other hand..."

She gripped him and began to massage.

Then she started kissing his chest, biting his nipples, moving lower, and lower still. Alex closed his eyes and let all coherent thought fade away.

She made it to his cock and drew him into her mouth again. Soft satin lips caressed, teased, worked him toward climax all too quickly. But then she slowed down, dragged her teeth gently along his length until he squirmed and shuddered and couldn't take another second of not being inside her.

"Stop," he said, gasping.

"You don't like?"

"I like," he whispered as he reached for another condom, opened the package and slid it on. "I definitely like."

He liked it too damn much.

He grasped her arms and tugged her up on top of him. Gripping her ass and shifting her hips, he buried his cock between her legs and pushed himself inside her. She was hot, sweet, wet and tight, even better the morning after.

For the first time since he'd set this crazy plan into motion, he understood the biggest danger of all. It wasn't Yasmine discovering his true identity. It was the danger of never wanting to let her go.

YASMINE COULDN'T REMEMBER the last time she'd felt so thoroughly satisfied. And if the rest of the weekend proved to be anything like the past twelve hours, she might never want to let Kyle out of bed.

But then, keeping him as her love slave definitely would be breaking some kind of law, crossing a line she'd never be able to cross. A girl could dream, anyway.

She was about to step into the shower with Kyle, who was already there, lathered up and looking even better wet than he did dry, when she heard her cell phone ringing in the next room. Only a few people had her number and knew not to call unless it was completely necessary, so she hurried to answer.

"Hello?" she said after she'd dug the phone out of her purse, gripping the towel around herself.

"It's Cass. I need you to fix my computer, ASAP."

"You're calling my cell phone about your *computer?* Is this an actual emergency?"

"Yes!"

"Um, I'm kind of tied up right now," she said, glancing at Kyle standing dripping wet and naked in the bathroom doorway now, threatening to make her forget how to string words into coherent sentences.

"Please help me! I've got that dinner party tonight, and all the recipes I want to use are on the Internet."

"And?"

"And when I try to log on, nothing happens. No Internet!"

Any other time Yasmine would have been a little more tolerant of Cass's computer ineptitude, but this time she expelled a noisy sigh and said, "I'm sorry I can't help. Maybe you should buy a cookbook."

"You're just going to leave me hanging? On Christmas Eve? Your best friend?"

Drew popped into her head—Drew, whom she knew would be a great guy for Cass. If Cass could overlook the slightly nerdy appearance to see the nice guy beneath.

"I've got a friend who lives not too far from you and might be free to help you out. I could call him and ask."

"Please, please, please?"

"On one condition."

"Anything—you name it."

"If he fixes your computer, you ask him out on a date."

Silence. And then Cass said, "Okay, what's the matter with this guy that he needs you bribing women to go out with him?"

"He's the guy I mentioned to you. He's nice. Give him a chance."

"I told you, I don't do nerds."

"That's my condition. You ask him out, go on a date with him, give him a real chance or no computer help for you."

"I had no idea you could play so dirty."

"Like I said, you could go buy a cookbook."

"I had all my recipes picked out and bookmarked on that cooking Web site you showed me."

"Should have printed them, huh?"

Yasmine bit her lip to keep from laughing. Kyle was leaning against the door frame now with his arms crossed over his chest, half-smiling as he listened to her conversation. Oddly, she liked him listening in. She found it somehow familiar and intimate in a way she hadn't been with a guy in too long.

Cass, apparently finished stewing, sighed. "Fine. If he can come fix my computer, I'll ask him out. And if he's cute, I'll take him to bed and screw his brains out."

"No charity sex. Just be open to possibilities, okay? If he's home, I'll have him call you and set up a time to come over. If he's not available, I'll call you back."

She hung up with Cass and gave Kyle an apologetic smile. "I'll be finished in a sec."

"Playing matchmaker?"

She shrugged. "I promised Drew I'd hook him up, and as you can see from his date last night, he needs all the help he can get."

"I'll be waiting in the tub—hurry up," he said as he gave her a once-over. "Lose the towel."

Yasmine dialed Drew's number, and luckily he picked up. In a mere two minutes, she'd confirmed he was free and set him up to meet Cass. Satisfied that her matchmaker work was done for the day, she turned off her cell phone to save herself any more unwelcome interruptions and headed for the bathroom.

An hour and a steamy round of shower sex later, Yasmine and Kyle were clean and dressed, rejuvenated by doughnuts and coffee, and pulling into a parking spot in front of Yasmine's apartment. She couldn't think what they'd do or talk about all day if not for sex, but hey, if sex was all they had in common, she'd be the last girl to complain. Because it was really, really good.

Outside the car, houses in her neighborhood glinted here and there with Christmas lights, while just as many were decidedly unfestive looking. Her own building, a blue and green Victorian that had long ago been converted to four puny apartments, was one of the unfestive variety, since it was inhabited by a Buddhist couple, a pagan and two lazy singles—including Yasmine—who couldn't be bothered with decorations.

She had an odd sense that she'd embarked on some kind of escape from reality with Kyle, as though she was seeing her own neighborhood with the fresh eyes of a tourist. And maybe that's what she needed to break out of the doldrums that had settled on her lately—a wild little escape from reality. Maybe this change of perspective would appease her bad-girl urges and she'd be able to return to her rule-following, law-abiding—albeit boring—life with no more tempting whispers from that quarter.

Or maybe she'd just finally be able to finish her current software project with a renewed sense of creativity.

She led Kyle up the stairs and into her apartment, feeling a tiny bit embarrassed that she hadn't even gotten a tabletop tree.

"So this is my place," she said, making a sweeping motion.

The cinnamon-colored walls, the iron grillwork she'd arranged as wall decor, the purple sofa, the middle-eastern fabrics draped over the tables and arm of the sofa—it all added up to a warm, cozy place that was distinctly hers. She loved her apartment, small and creaky as it was, and she'd worked her ass off making it a home.

"Nice," Kyle said as he surveyed the living room. "Makes my place look like a crap hole."

She tried not to laugh but failed. "Maybe you could use a little decorating help—not that I'm volunteering for the job or anything. You can pay people to do that for you."

Her Siamese cat, Milo, darted out from his perch on the window and raced across the room, skidding to a stop in the kitchen doorway. He looked up at her with his haughty blue eyes and yowled.

"He's trying to convince me he nearly starved to death during my absence."

"Hey, kitty," Kyle said as he crouched down and extended his hand to the cat, who in turn stood up on his hind legs and swatted at Kyle's hand.

"Milo, behave!" She said to the cat, and to Kyle, "Don't worry, I got him at the shelter and his previous owner had his claws removed. He can bite, but he lives under the delusion that he's still a fierce, clawed warrior."

She went to the kitchen and filled the cat's bowls with food and water, then returned to find Milo still with Kyle, letting him stroke his back.

"Wow, you should feel privileged."

He shrugged. "Animals like me."

"So do women," she said as he stood up. She slid her hands around his waist and pressed her body against him.

"I'm mainly concerned about one particular woman right now."

"Oh? Well, the one I know of is liking you really, really well."

He cast a glance at the gifts she'd brought in from the car for him that he still hadn't opened. "I was going to suggest you put those under the tree, but there's not a tree. Do you have maybe a house plant or something we could decorate?"

"We should get a tree, you think? To celebrate properly?"

Kyle gave her a look. "That *is* the tradition."

"I didn't see any point in putting one up if it was just going to be for me."

"But add a person, and you gotta have a tree."

"Right. I think there's a lot a few blocks over that's selling live trees. This late in the game, though, we might get stuck with the Charlie Brown variety."

Given Yasmine's sad little collection of leftover ornaments that she hadn't used in her cubicle, acquired as gifts from various people over the years and mostly not removed from their original packaging, an ugly tree was better—it would keep her ornaments from looking so pathetic.

"Maybe we can find a little tabletop one," she said.

"Oh come on, I like a nice, big tree. Maybe an eight- or nine-footer."

She looked at him as though he'd lost it. "Are you decorating the White House or my apartment?"

"Okay, let's say we see what kind of selection is left."

"We might also want to grab lunch out. My apartment is sadly lacking in the food department."

"That cat food smell is giving me a weird craving," Kyle said.

Yasmine wrinkled her nose. "For what? Horse meat?"

"For clam chowder in those sourdough bowls like the tourists eat down at Fisherman's Wharf."

"Cat food reminds you of *that?*"

"After we pick up a tree, want to take a streetcar there and be tourists today?"

"God, I can't remember the last time I was down there."

"And we could shop for some more gifts to put under the tree…."

Yasmine smiled at the idea of taking a streetcar and playing tourists. "Should we put on white sneakers and jeans and I 'heart' San Francisco T-shirts so we'll blend in with the crowd?"

He made a face. "I wouldn't go that far."

"Promise to buy me a San Francisco snow globe, and you've got yourself a date."

6

CASS LIKED TO COOK once in a while, but she had to admit, her culinary concoctions didn't always turn out the way she hoped. Hosting her first dinner party in months, she'd fully intended to produce not a single disaster dish for her friends by planning ahead and sticking closely to the recipes. But now, thanks to procrastination, her whole stupid plan was going to hell.

And if this Drew guy turned out to be a toad, Yasmine would pay. The doorbell rang, and Cassandra checked her appearance in the mirror on her way to answer. Not that she felt too concerned about impressions—she'd seen a few of the computer monkeys Yasmine worked with.

Peering through her peephole, her subconscious began to calculate exactly how much her best friend would have to pay, but her mental calculator halted on the plus sign.

The guy on the other side was tall, thin, with shaggy brown hair in need of a good cut. He wore a pair of wire-rim glasses, and it didn't look as though he'd shaved yet today. Still, he wasn't bad looking.

Further inspection revealed that he was wearing a red-and-green flannel shirt that looked way too Paul Bunyan for Cass's taste, and was so new and starchy he'd probably ripped the sale tag off it a half hour ago.

That's what he'd chosen to wear to impress her? It must have been his effort at looking festive, and she had to give him credit for trying. She even felt a little sense of affection that he'd gotten spiffed up for her in his finest logging apparel.

She accepted her questionable fate and opened the door. "Hi, Drew. Thank you so much for coming over— and on Christmas Eve."

He smiled and extended a hand, which she accepted in an awkward handshake.

"No problem. Yasmine said you were desperate."

Cass imagined her best friend telling this guy that she was lonely and horny, that she hadn't had a decent date all month and hadn't come within shouting distance of a live, naked penis in longer than she cared to admit.

He seemed to realize his mistake. "Oh, I mean, desperate to get your computer fixed. Not, you know…desperate for anything else."

A surprised laugh burst out of her, easing the tension in the air.

"Come on in," she said. "I'll try not to look too desperate."

She led him to the traitorous computer from hell, which always managed to conk out on her at the most inopportune times, such as when she was in need of a midnight shoe-shopping binge or a midafternoon perusal of hot guy pics on the Internet.

"So what seems to be the problem? Something about the Internet not working?"

Cass told him about the error message she was getting, and he nodded as he checked something on the back of the CPU. Seeming to be satisfied with what was going on back there in the never-never land of cables and cords, he sat down, then started rambling on in techno-babble as he typed and clicked his way through various screens.

She mmm-hmmed and nodded as if she had a clue what he was talking about, then made an excuse about something she needed to check in the kitchen. Alone in the midst of her self-created domestic purgatory, she rummaged around in the fridge pretending to have a purpose. Her only real agenda was to stay away from Drew while she tried to think of some suitable reason to tell Yasmine why she couldn't ask him out.

Such as he wore a Paul Bunyan shirt and talked so fast and about such dull things she could hardly understand him. Maybe she'd be fibbing a bit on the second part, but she was pretty sure he'd prove her right, given enough time. He definitely didn't seem like the kind of guy who'd go for an over-the-hill ex-stripper. She'd probably have to go trolling the late-night leftovers at her favorite nightclubs to find those guys—so it was a good thing she didn't really want a guy at all.

After rummaging around the kitchen for as long as she reasonably could, she poked her head out the doorway and asked, "Can I get you something to drink?"

"No, thanks," Drew said. "I think I've got your problem fixed."

"Wow, already?"

"Sometimes computers just sort of freak out and need to be turned off for ten seconds and restarted. That should be the first thing you try if you can't figure out what's wrong."

"Oh," she said, entering the living room again. "I think Yasmine has told me to do that before. I just forgot."

"Not a big deal." He opened up her Web browser, and there it was—the Internet back and waiting to tell her how to make parmesan stuffed mushrooms.

"You're welcome to stay for a drink. I've got to get started on cooking right away though," she said as she sat down at her desk.

"Thanks, but I'd better go. I have a family thing to attend today."

"Ugh, family. I actually miss them this time of year— they're all in Santa Barbara, and I didn't feel like flying down there again for the weekend. So I'm having some friends over for dinner instead."

She looked at him, and for the first time, noticed that he had a nice smile.

"I was wondering," she said before she could change her mind, "if you'd like to go out sometime. I could take you to dinner as a thank-you for fixing my computer."

He waved away her suggestion. "All I did was restart it. That's not worth a meal."

Boy was this guy dense. "So come to dinner, anyway."

He blinked behind his glasses, and Cass was tempted to add, please don't wear that shirt.

He flashed a crooked smile and shrugged. "Okay, why not?"

"How about Monday night? Are you free then?" Better to get the deed over with sooner rather than later was Cass's philosophy.

Drew appeared to give the matter some thought, probably trying to decide whether a night with her would be more exciting than a night of Internet porn, or whatever guys like him spent their time doing.

"I think I'm free. I mean, well…actually, I know I'm free."

"Perfect. So why don't you pick me up around six?"

"Yeah, um, sure. So, we'll go to dinner."

"I'd invite you to stay for dinner tonight, but you said you have family plans."

Another shrug. "Yeah, I do."

"You sure about that drink? You could keep me company while I cook." She surprised herself with the insistence that he stay.

For whatever silly reason, she wanted companionship—anyone's, apparently.

"Sure, some water would be great."

"Let me just print these recipes, and I'll be all set."

Five minutes later she was wrist deep in the stuffing for her mushrooms, and Drew was busy hollowing out the mushrooms' centers, even after she'd insisted he didn't need to help. He'd claimed he couldn't sit still and watch other people work, so she'd given in.

"You cook at home?" she asked.

"Not much. I'm always forgetting some important ingredient. Guess I don't have the patience to be a great cook."

"And I don't have what it takes to be a computer genius."

"So have you and Yasmine been friends long?" he asked.

"We met in college. I was a struggling grad student, and she was a prodigy acing all her classes without cracking a book."

"A grad student. Let me guess—business? International relations?"

"Am I that obvious? I earned my MBA with lots of blood, sweat and tears."

If he knew she'd really spent most of her college years working as a stripper, he'd have seen her in a totally different and not nearly so pleasant light. Cass saved that bit of information for her closest friends and confidantes—a category where the men in her life simply didn't fit.

"So what do you do now?"

"I'm VP of marketing at an investment company downtown."

"Wow, a vice president. Do you have your own office and everything?"

"Of course." She glanced over and caught an odd smile on his lips. "What?"

He looked at her, and his smile faded. "Oh nothing."

"No, really, you were smiling. You probably think I'm a cliché, don't you? The stereotypical career-driven female with no time for a life."

"Not at all. I swear, I wasn't thinking anything like that, and clearly have a life."

"Then tell me what you *were* thinking." Definitely the earliest Cass had ever made that request of a guy, and probably a welcome kiss-of-death for this doomed flirtation.

"I was thinking, it's really sexy that you're a high-powered career woman with your own office."

She laughed, but secretly she was flattered.

"You think?" Cass had always considered the whole female exec thing pretty sexy, too, but she'd never heard a man express the sentiment.

"Guess I've got a thing for women in powerful places."

Cass stared at the glob of mushroom stuffing she'd formed in the bowl. She'd been mixing it furiously with her hands as they talked, and now it was ready to be used as filling for the mushroom caps. But her mind was a million miles from finger foods. It occurred to her then that what Drew had said about her job wasn't just flattering. It was an incredible...turn-on.

Her plans to ditch Drew at the earliest opportunity weren't sounding so great now. In fact, she was beginning to wonder what lay beneath his unpolished exterior. Could computer geeks be sexy, too? Never one to shy away from the big questions, she decided to face the matter head-on.

Cass's hands were covered in stuffing, and she brushed them off as best she could. Then she scooped up a glob with her finger and closed the distance between herself and Drew. "Want a taste?"

He spun around, and she nearly pinned him between herself and the counter. "Um, sure," he said, looking a little perplexed by her proximity.

Up close he had a thoroughly male presence, and she was only a few inches away, close enough that if she shifted her hips, she'd bump against him.

She lifted her finger to his mouth, and it occurred to her only then that he might be one of those fussy guys with hygiene issues. If she had to point out to him that she'd washed her hands before diving into the mushroom stuffing—

But she didn't.

He took her hand in his and guided her finger into

his mouth, then let his tongue caress it, lingering and tasting long enough to make her panties wet. He may have had no fashion sense, but he knew how to work over a finger. And if he knew how to work her there...

Cass slid her finger from his mouth, then caught the look of confusion in his eyes, and she flashed a smile.

"Thanks," she whispered.

"For cleaning your finger off?"

"Yeah."

"Tastes good," he said. "The stuffing, I mean."

There was a pause, not exactly an awkward one. Cass suddenly wanted a better feel for his lips. When he kissed, did he use his tongue as well as he did when licking a finger? She looked at his mouth and tried to imagine kissing him. Surprisingly, it was an easy fantasy to conjure.

She decided that on their date, instead of giving him a quick heave-ho—unless Drew turned into an obnoxious dork—she would satisfy her curiosity.

Cass tried to make sense of the fact that she was completely horny for a guy who lacked obviously sexy physical attributes. Unlike Yasmine, she liked her men gorgeous and hard-bodied. She didn't go for subtleties, not in any part of her life, but with Drew... His appeal was all about subtlety.

"What's wrong?" Drew asked.

"Um, nothing." She produced a fake-sounding laugh.

"What was that?"

"A finger licking?"

"I know what it *was*. I mean—"

"How did we go from making stuffed mushrooms to you sucking my finger? I don't know."

Except, she did know. There wasn't anything like sex to distract a guy from getting serious or playing the getting-to-know-you game or pretty much anything else. The last thing she needed was to complicate her newfound happiness with another relationship. But she would hate to turn down a little action in her sex life.

From somewhere in the region of Drew's ass, a little bell rang. Cass looked at his pants, an old pair of khakis, as he reached into his back pocket and pulled out a digital organizer.

"Sorry," he said, as he flipped open the top. He read the screen and said, "I'm supposed to be at a family get-together in twenty minutes. Guess I'd better be going."

"Thanks for stopping by," she said as she took a step back and gave him some distance. "I'll see you Monday?"

"Definitely."

Cass smiled. "Have a merry Christmas."

"You, too," Drew said as he stepped out the door, then turned to look at her. "And call me if you have any more computer problems."

When she was alone in the apartment again, she looked at her crusty hands and sighed. For a crazy moment she'd been tempted to abandon her boyfriend-free happiness for the mysteries of the unknown with a guy who wasn't her type.

She didn't want to like Drew, but she did want to get laid. She didn't really want him to be too into her, and yet she found herself wanting to impress him. Clearly, she needed to get a grip.

Cass had just flirted with her first nerd, and the experience hadn't even been remotely unpleasant. She might have even called it a pleasure.

7

YASMINE GAZED UP at the pointy top of the eight-foot-tall Christmas tree. "You've got to be kidding."

Kyle looked from the supersize tree to her. "What?"

"For one thing, we can't carry that all the way home. And for another, it would take up my entire living room."

"Oh, right. Well, how about that one?" He pointed to a tree that was maybe two feet shorter.

"Think tabletop." Yasmine turned and headed for the smallest trees on the lot.

Twenty feet away, on the other side of a chain-link fence, the roar of traffic was a constant reminder that they were still in the city and not an evergreen forest. A car horn honked, a seagull squawked overhead and the scent of car exhaust filled the air. Ah, urban life. Yasmine loved it.

She caught Kyle's look of disdain as he peered down at the little tree she'd stopped in front of. "What?"

"It's just so...small."

"What is it about guys and tree size? It's like some kind of phallic thing."

"Freud was a crackpot."

"I promise, the size of your tree doesn't in any way reflect on the size of your manhood. Okay?"

He rolled his eyes at her and strolled over to the next

biggest tree. "Did you do this with your parents as a kid? Go pick out a tree every year?"

"A few times, but since we spent most of our holidays in Paris, we normally didn't have a tree."

"No Christmas tree? Where did Santa leave presents?"

"In our stockings. We always packed those and took them to France every year, and since whatever we got had to fit in our suitcase for the flight home, I always got tiny gifts."

"We went out to the woods and chopped down trees when I was really little. Later we had a fake tree, one of those perfectly cone-shaped ones with branches so unbendable you could hang bowling balls on it for ornaments."

Yasmine tried to imagine Kyle as a little boy and couldn't. She spotted a cute little tree without any major holes and pointed to it. "How about this one?"

He shrugged. "Sure, I guess if you want to prove size doesn't matter."

She caught the attention of an employee clad in a green apron, and then they stood waiting for him to help them. "Do you have siblings?"

Part of her wanted to know everything about Kyle, and another part of her just wanted to keep him vague and anonymous, not another guy she could fall for only to find that he was more enamored with her outside than her inside.

"An older brother and a younger sister. We fought all the time growing up, but we're friends now."

"I've always envied people with siblings, but I guess I had it pretty easy, not having to compete for attention or Christmas presents or anything."

"It must have been lonely sometimes, being an only child." He looked at her as if he were seeing her for the first time, and Yasmine got a ridiculous little chill.

She tightened her long green scarf and tugged her denim jacket closed against the damp, cool air. Overhead, clouds formed a dense white blanket.

"I had nannies who were usually lots of fun. Leave it to my mom to hire the very best. But when I saw other kids at the playground with their siblings, I always told myself someday my parents would have more kids. I had this whole imaginary family made up in my head."

The tree lot employee arrived, and Kyle told him which tree they wanted. He gave them a claim tag for it, and as he took it to the register for them, they went to the huge line that snaked through the left side of the lot and waited.

"I always thought I'd have at least two kids so neither of them would be lonely or have to make up imaginary families," Kyle said, and Yasmine felt a stab of dread that they'd entered that precarious territory few couples ventured into unless they were getting serious—the kids discussion.

Definitely not a talk to have with a weekend fling.

"I had a sister named Angelina, and a brother named Blaize, and another sister named Anastasia. They were all younger than me, and they all did whatever I told them to do." Yasmine deliberately kept her tone light to steer the conversation away from serious territory.

"Those are pretty fancy names."

"Hey, I was a kid who read a lot and watched too much TV. I think Blaize was a soap opera character at the time."

"What about you? Do you want to have your own kids someday?"

Whoa, there—too much, too fast. Yasmine's stomach knotted.

"I, um, haven't really thought about it."

"Who hasn't thought about having kids?"

She raised her hand. "Me! Me!"

"So your goal in life is just to work at a virtual-sex software company and live in an apartment alone?"

"Pretty much, yeah." She smiled, but her heart wasn't in it, and she was afraid Kyle could tell.

Yasmine had given up on having big, lofty goals somewhere along the way. She'd decided while serving her time in juvenile detention that when she got out, she'd just be happy with whatever life presented her. She didn't think there would be much point in expecting big things from her future, careerwise, and somehow she'd come to have the same low expectations of her personal life.

"Judging by your reputation at work, it seems like you're capable of running your own software company instead of just being a programmer for one."

She shrugged. "I'm not much of a business person."

Kyle flashed her an odd look but said nothing more. A few seconds later, they'd made it to the cash register, and he insisted on paying for the tree. He propped it on his shoulder for the walk home.

"You look so outdoorsy with that tree slung over your shoulder," she said as they crossed the street.

"Oh, yeah? Are you into the outdoorsy look?"

"I didn't think so, but it works for you." She let her gaze travel from his eyes downward, over his broad chest to his waist and below.

He slipped his free arm around her waist, and she felt his finger hook into her belt loop. The gesture seemed more intimate somehow than she was prepared for, and she had to resist the urge to pull away. She was truly a person with issues when she could sleep with a guy, but when he slipped his finger into her belt loop, all of a sudden she was feeling freaked.

Clearly, she needed help.

"What's wrong?" Kyle asked, surprisingly attuned to her mood changes.

"Oh, nothing. Guess I'm just getting hungry for lunch." Which wasn't exactly a lie.

"Can you make it until we get down to the wharf, or do you need to eat now?"

Yasmine must have been desperate for affection, because that one little gesture of concern for her well-being nearly melted her heart. "I guess I can hold out for clam chowder in a sourdough bowl."

They made it back to her apartment, dropped off the tree and headed out for the streetcar stop a block away.

As an adult, Yasmine drove everywhere. She hadn't taken a streetcar probably since her teen years. And standing at the corner, without warning, her chest filled up with a strange longing for something she couldn't name.

Something about Kyle and the streetcars and this little escape from reality they seemed to have embarked upon made her think too much about the past, about the things she couldn't change. But she couldn't let that crap get her down now. She owed herself a weekend of pure escapist fantasy, and she was determined to enjoy every fleeting moment of it.

THE STREET CAR stopped on The Embarcadero not far from Fisherman's Wharf, and Alex reminded himself for the hundredth time why he was with Yasmine. Not to have fun, and not to forget all his problems, but to find out if she was still a hacker. He'd suggested they go on their little tourist excursion as a way to gain her trust, to get her to let her guard down in a completely different environment than the one in which she usually lived. But it was just so damn easy to lose himself in her company, and he had to admit, he was thoroughly enjoying playing the tourist in his adopted city for the first time.

During the ride to the waterfront, they took in the scenery together, probably looking to all the world like a pair of happy lovers. He felt more comfortable with Yasmine than he should have, and he liked her more than he should have. She was more comfortable in her own skin than most of the women he'd ever known, and her comfort with herself made it easy for others to be at ease with her.

He couldn't help thinking, in another time, another place, maybe they could have been a real couple. But as soon as the thought formed in his head, he banished it. He knew too well the dangers of wanting what he couldn't have.

When they reached their final stop, Alex stepped off the street car and extended his hand to Yasmine as she stepped down, too. The weather here was a little windier than it had been at her place, and he was glad now that he'd worn a heavy leather jacket and his flannel-lined jeans. The scent of the ocean mingled with the less pleasant odor of sea lions, and as they crossed onto the sidewalk, they had to keep moving to avoid blocking the steady stream of tourists milling through.

"Where to?" he asked Yasmine once they had a chance to stop and get their bearings.

"Toward the smell of food."

They wandered a row of seafood vendors until they found one with the best looking bowls, then crossed the street with their sourdough bowls and colds cans of Coke and sat on a concrete platform where people, seagulls and pigeons gathered for lunch. A particularly large seagull landed a few feet away from them and stood eyeing their food, while the less aggressive birds nervously edged closer a few inches at a time.

"You think he'll attack?" Alex asked.

"It's not a matter of 'if' so much as 'when.' We'd better eat fast."

He looked over and caught Yasmine tossing the seagull a piece of bread. "Isn't that illegal or something?"

"Shh. I'm buying us time."

He stole another glimpse of her and his heart swelled in his chest. He'd never wanted a woman so much as he wanted her then, sitting beside him on this cool, damp day. And he'd never been a bigger fool in his life. How had he turned physical desire into emotional desire overnight?

Okay, so it was a natural progression, but he'd been a fool not to anticipate it, not to realize he wasn't the kind of guy who slept with women indiscriminately. He'd always considered sex a small part of the big picture in relationships.

He focused on the hot chowder and tried to let the more troubling thoughts vacate his mind, but no luck. By the time he'd emptied the bread bowl and started breaking off pieces of it to eat, the thought that he was getting too emotionally involved with Yasmine could not be ignored.

"You look so serious," she said. She'd finished her soup now and was breaking off more pieces of it and tossing them to the birds. Pigeons scampered around her sexy black boots, hoping to be the next recipient of her goodwill.

Alex forced a smile and took a drink of his Coke. "Just worried that one of these birds is going to dive bomb us if we don't get moving soon."

Had he really been stupid enough to think he could resolve ten years of wanting with a few nights of great sex? Had he really believed the situation wouldn't get any more complicated than it already was?

Damn it, he had. Maybe deep down, he'd known he would be walking into a no-win situation, but he'd fooled himself.

Having tossed her last bit of bread and finished her drink, Yasmine gazed at the row of cheesy tourist shops lining the street across from where they sat. "I think we have to buy some T-shirts, don't we? Isn't that the rule if you come down here—you have to leave with a shirt that declares your love for San Francisco?"

"I'm no expert."

"How about, I'll pick out a shirt for you, and you pick one out for me?"

"How about we just skip the T-shirt thing? I thought we were shopping for snow globes."

"Don't try to distract me with plastic trinkets," Yasmine said as she took his hand and tugged him toward the strip of shops. "I'm buying a shirt, and that's final."

Her hand in his felt right as they walked, felt like the kind of comfort he hadn't realized he'd been wanting for a long time. He glanced over at her and was struck by the sensation that she recognized him. Fear shot through him, but he did his best to show no emotion.

"What?" he said when she continued to stare at him.

"It's weird," she said as they waited at the traffic light to cross. "I occasionally get the feeling we've known each other before."

"Maybe we've bumped into each other around town somewhere. I jog in Golden Gate Park pretty often, usually around Stowe Lake."

Had she detected the slight note of tension in his voice that he'd failed to hide?

"I doubt that's it. I just can't think where we might have met."

Alex's stomach churned as he scrambled for a way to change the subject. His gaze settled on the nearest shop, its entrance crowded with racks of T-shirts and its display window filled with trinkets, including snow globes. "Looks like we've found our destination," he said.

It worked—instant distraction. Yasmine headed for the nearest rack and grabbed a bright-orange shirt that read 'Orange you glad I visited San Francisco?"

She held it up and smiled. "This is perfect for you."

"That's the dumbest T-shirt I've ever seen."

"Exactly. Now you have to find an even worse one for me."

Alex gave her a look, but she draped the shirt over her arm and wandered farther into the store. He wanted to find something to dislike about her, something that would bring him back to Earth and show him that no matter how perfect she seemed, she really was a common criminal.

He just needed a little more time. Another day or two would be enough for him to dig up the truth. Either that or fall head over heels in love.

WHO KNEW DECORATING a tree could turn into such an erotic undertaking?

Yasmine watched the tiny white lights twinkling and felt for a moment as though she was a little girl again, filled with the excitement of Christmas Eve. All the possibilities, the promise of goodies to come, the mystery of presents to be puzzled over and opened.

But then she remembered she was lying naked next to a guy she'd known less than a month, and the evening took on a whole different sense of possibility.

After an afternoon of wandering the shops and sites around the Wharf and Pier 39, they'd returned to Yasmine's apartment and set about decorating the tree, a task that had resulted in each of them getting more undressed for every item of clothing that the tree put on.

"I don't want to hear a word about my ornaments," she said when she caught him looking at the tree, a smile playing on his lips.

"I didn't say anything." He looked at the cat, perched on the back of the table next to them. "Did you hear me say anything?"

Milo blinked at him.

"You were about to critique, I could tell."

"I'm just awed by your creativity, that's all."

She'd seen a decorating show that used household objects as nontraditional tree decorations and had insisted

on trying it herself instead of hauling out her collection
of ugly rejected ornaments. So now the tree was bedecked
in scarves and belts, earrings and pendants, ribbons and
tassels. It looked a little odd, but kind of fun, too.

"Yeah, well. At least you're a man who knows when
to stick with the safe response."

"Especially when I have a beautiful woman lying naked next to me." He pulled the blanket from the back of
the couch over them and wrapped his arms around her.

Kyle may have been a guy she barely knew, but this
was turning out to be the most fun Christmas Eve she'd
had since the days of believing in Santa Claus. Then the
phone rang, interrupting their perfect moment for the
second time that day.

Yasmine reached over him to the cordless phone on
the end table and answered, barely able to concentrate
on "Hello" when she had Kyle's chest to ponder up
close and personal.

"Yasmine? It's Cass. Where the hell are you?"

"I'm home, obviously, and your timing today is incredibly bad."

"You forgot my party."

"Your party… Oh, right. I told you weeks ago I didn't
want to go," Yasmine said as she glanced at Kyle.

"And I told you to get your ass over here, anyway."

"I thought you were joking."

"I never joke about yuletide events."

"I guess this means Drew fixed your computer and
you were able to let loose in the kitchen." Which was a
scary thought, given Cass's level of culinary skill.

"Yes, and thanks for sending him. But seriously, I'll
be the only single here if you don't show."

Yasmine winced. Cass had been dating her last boy-friend when she'd planned the party, and he'd broken up with her soon after.

"Listen, I'm actually kind of tied up right now." Tied up—now there was something she and Kyle hadn't tried yet…. Where were those furry handcuffs, anyway?

"Watching the MTV Christmas special does not qualify as holiday plans."

"No, I mean, I have company right now."

Silence. And then, "Oh! You have male company. Who is it?"

"No one you know."

"You're being uncharacteristically coy— Wait a min-ute, it's not that guy from your office that you bought handcuffs and candy for, is it?"

"It is," Yasmine said, trying to reveal too much to Kyle. He didn't need to know she'd had conversations with friends about him.

"And let me guess. He's lying right there naked be-side you."

"Um…"

"Yasmine! You slut, I was joking."

"So you can understand why I won't be attending your party."

"No, what I understand is why you'll be getting your ass over here within the hour. I made a Yule log for you. With decorative leaves and chocolate filling. You *will* be here to partake. Do you understand?"

"Oh God, Cass, you shouldn't have. I was joking about the log."

She'd told her friend the thing she'd missed most

about her childhood Christmas vacations in Paris was the *bûche de Noël*. Her parents had always bought one at a *pâtisserie* near the flat where they stayed, and they'd always let her have the biggest piece of the chocolate log-shaped cake. When Cass had issued the invitation to her all-couples-except-Yasmine Christmas Eve party, Yasmine had jokingly said she would only show if there was a big chocolate Yule log in her honor.

"You're lucky I forgot to start cooking the turkey on time—dinner's in an hour. You and the office hottie had better be here. Got it?"

"Really, Cass. I don't think that's a good idea. And besides—"

"No excuses. You have no idea what a pain in the ass this Yule log was."

"But..." Yasmine scrambled to think of a new excuse, unwilling as she was to get out of bed at the moment. "He doesn't believe in celebrating Christmas. He's a...Moonie."

"So he can pretend there's not a tree and enjoy the merriment anyway. Really, babe, this is a multicultural, multifaith affair."

Yasmine gave Kyle a look pregnant with warning as she said goodbye to Cass and then reached across him again to hang up the phone.

"That was my best friend," she said. "She's insisting we show up at her Christmas Eve party, which is already in session and which she apparently was expecting me to attend even after I said I wouldn't be there."

Kyle glanced down at his still-present erection. "Do you think we have time—"

"If we're fast," she said as she straddled his hips and connected their bodies.

"I can do fast," he said.

And he could. Remarkably well.

Fifteen minutes later they were both breathless and satisfied, tugging on their clothes and getting themselves looking presentable.

They set off on the eight-block walk to Cass's apartment in the cool darkness, hand in hand. While Yasmine was happy to have a date, she was a little weirded out by their fast physical comfort. And that holding hands freaked her out more than having sex with him told Yasmine once again that she had definitely gotten her perspective knocked askew.

Instead of examining her problem closer, she opted to prepare Kyle for his impending immersion into her social group.

"Be warned," she said as they waited for a light to change so they could cross the street. "My friends have mostly settled into happy coupledom. They tend to view singles like us as potential converts, and they see it as their personal directive to spread the gospel of commitment and marriage."

"And you're opposed to the whole concept?" he said with a half-smile.

"Well, no. I just think we're all a bit young to be getting too serious."

"I guess that's my problem. I'm already over the hill, eh?"

She laughed. "You've been holding your own in the bedroom for being such a geriatric patient."

"Smart-ass."

"So what we're doing isn't too serious for you?"

"Definitely not. But if I find out you're sleeping with me just to research some new sex software—"

"Oh no, you've found me out! Whatever you do, don't ever try the upcoming game entitled Old Guy Sex."

He gave her a swat on the backside. "How did you end up working at VirtualActive? You don't exactly fit the profile of the typical employee."

"Yeah, well. Being a notorious former hacker doesn't endear me to potential employers."

"A *what?*"

"A hacker, cracker, system intruder—whatever you want to call it. You probably saw me on the news and don't remember. I was the first teen hacker given more than a slap on the wrist for accessing government computers."

"You? I don't believe it."

She shrugged. "It's true. I was stupid. I had no idea how much trouble I was getting myself into. I just thought of it as an interesting puzzle to solve."

"So you were just breaking into these computers to see if you could do it?"

"Yeah, it's not like I was stealing information or anything."

"And they sent you to prison? That's harsh," he said, sounding outraged by the whole idea.

"It's behind me. I don't think about it much anymore. If I start thinking, I get pissed off."

"What was being in juvenile prison like?"

"It sucked. I mean, think about it—there aren't a lot of opportunities for white-collar teen crime. The kids I was in with were there for violent crimes, drug-related stuff, gang banging… It was a far cry from my old private girls' school crowd."

"So what did you do?"

"I suffered through, avoided eye contact, got my ass beat now and then."

"That must have been awful…. Now that you mention it, I think I do remember seeing your story on the news. What did your parents think?"

"They were horrified that I'd broken the law, and they thought I deserved whatever punishment the court gave me."

"That's harsh."

"That's my good old ma and pa. Always on my side through thick and thin."

"You get along better with them now?"

"Not exactly. We have our arguments, but mainly I've never totally forgiven them for not being a little more supportive back then."

They walked in silence for a short while, and Yasmine began to wonder if she'd freaked him out to the point of silence.

Finally he spoke up again, and she breathed a sigh of relief. "Did you ever think about not becoming a programmer—maybe doing something outside the technical industry?"

Yasmine shrugged. "No. I applied to what felt like a hundred companies, and VirtualActive is the one that hired me."

"No surprise there. For an office full of guys who sit around creating virtual sex games all day, you provide some pretty hot inspiration."

"Ew."

"Don't tell me you've never realized that."

"I did—I mean, I do, but I try not to think about it."

"What about the heroine in Jungle Honey? Don't you think she looks eerily similar to you?"

Yasmine laughed, her cheeks burning at the sudden realization that he was right. "Oh…my…God. We came out with that game about six months after I was hired."

"You see? It was just a matter of months before they put you in a furry leopard-print bikini and had you tying unsuspecting tourists up with vines in the jungle."

"And acting out kinky sex acts with them."

"And with bananas."

"Crap." She covered her face with her hands and tried not to remember who exactly had been on that software development team.

"You don't plan to spend the rest of your life creating virtual sex software, do you?"

"What's wrong with that? Maybe it's my calling."

But it wasn't. She had no idea what her calling was. She could only say what it wasn't.

"You'd be wasting your talent."

"Hey," she said, forcing her face into a serious expression. "We create products that touch people's lives."

"Especially horny, dateless people."

"It's meaningful work."

"You're absolutely right," Kyle said. "It's only a matter of time before the Nobel Prize people figure that out and create a new award for work in simulated sex experiences."

"Ha-ha."

"Sorry, I had no idea you took your work so seriously."

"You're new to the business. You don't have a clue

how much time and effort I've put into creating realistic-looking male members."

"Mmm-hmm. You're right, I have no idea. That must be something you've had to study extensively firsthand."

"Truth be told, I haven't had nearly enough up-close, hands-on experience with real-life models lately."

"Maybe you've been spending too much time working, not enough time researching."

"Mmm. Want to be my research buddy?"

"Only if I get to do my own research, too," he said, waggling his eyebrows. "So you've been at VirtualActive since college? About four years?"

"Five years. I made it through college in three years instead of four."

"Oh, yeah? So you're a genius or something?"

"I'm just impatient, that's all."

"And modest. I've heard through the grapevine that you can write circles around all the other programmers in the office."

"Who's been telling lies about me?"

"You're like an urban legend. Yasmine Talbot, code-slinging superbabe."

A bubble of laughter burst out of her. "Stop. That is *not* how my co-workers see me."

But she knew he was right. It wasn't hard to become legendary among a bunch of guys whose lives—and in some cases sex lives—existed mostly within a computer.

"So what do we tell everyone at this party about us? That we're shacked up for the weekend?"

"How about that we're co-workers, and this is our second date—on Christmas Eve because we've both been orphaned by our selfish vacation-crazed families."

"Is that what we call this—dating?"

"We could say we're just screwing, but... I don't think there's an actual word for what we're doing—or if there is one, it's not something we should be saying in polite circles."

"So this Cass? She's your best friend?"

"Yes, and she's also on my shit list for making me leave my apartment tonight."

"I promise we can make up for lost time later."

She smiled. "I guess there's really no hurry, right?"

"Right. If we don't slow down a little, I'm going to be useless by tomorrow," Kyle said.

They reached Cass's building, and Yasmine led the way up the steps. They were ushered inside Cass's apartment by a woman Yasmine didn't recognize, and the place was filled with merry-looking couples.

Cass immediately spotted them hanging up their coats and headed over. "Hi! Nice to meet you," she said to Kyle, her smile plastered on and her tone relentlessly cheery.

This was a sure sign that she intended to corner him before the night was through and grill him about his intentions and his pedigree and pretty much anything else she could find out. Later, she'd spill it all to Yasmine like a cat bringing home a prize rodent for its master. Cass did this to all of Yasmine's dates.

Kyle smiled and shook her hand. "Thanks for having me over," he said, and it was clear Cass would have no trouble getting him to confess his entire history.

For now, though, she excused herself and hurried off to the sound of crashing pans in the kitchen.

"That better not be my *bûche de Noël*," Yasmine called after her.

She spotted a few friends talking near a sparkling Christmas tree and led Kyle in their direction. Would everyone be able to tell right away that they were imposters as a couple? That they were more familiar in bed than out?

She smiled and tried to think happy couple thoughts.

"Hey, Yasmine, I'm on your team for Trivial Pursuit," a woman she knew as Nora, from Cass's office, said. "She's a total brainiac," she added to her boyfriend, Lionel.

"I was hoping in the spirit of the holidays, we could skip the Trivial Pursuit for once," Cass called from the kitchen.

"With Yasmine, that's simply not an option," Nora said, and she was right. A party was not complete without at least one Trivial Pursuit game, and usually a major argument breaking out over a Trivial Pursuit game.

She introduced Kyle to the group, carefully avoiding giving any more information than his name. Everyone's gaze raked over him, and she could see a few of them trying to decide which question to ask first.

Nora, never one to tiptoe around the subject, dove right in. "So you two are dating?"

"Um, sort of," Yasmine said.

"How long?"

She glanced at Kyle, hoping he'd have a good lie for an answer.

"Just a short while," he said, smooth as could be.

He was cuter than her last boyfriend by a mile, and his casual J. Crew catalog style was far cooler than her previous guy's affection for black leather pants—which, for the record, could never be removed quickly enough in the heat of passion.

All her friends would probably size up Kyle and deem him the catch of a lifetime, The One, and when he disappeared from Yasmine's life in another few days or weeks, they'd spend the next ten years shaking their heads and secretly speculating on the exact reasons Yasmine was unable to hold on to men.

Likely they'd deem it related to her sordid past.

She could hold on to any guy she wanted, she supposed, if she actually wanted to keep him around. She glanced at Kyle and wondered if he had potential for more than just a weekend fling. He could hold a conversation, and he was smart and funny and great in bed, and her cat liked him. But there was that whole co-worker issue. And the fact that something about him haunted her, left her feeling as though she was hanging out with a ghost from her past.

It was one thing to have hot sex with a co-worker and then have to go about pretending it never happened. But it was quite another matter to get real emotions involved, have a relationship, let the world know they were a thing, and then break up and have to live with all that emotional baggage sitting in the middle of the office between them.

And could he see her as something more than a pretty face? Could he care about her as a person as much as he cared about the way she looked? Did she even care?

No, she'd take the weekend fling and be happy with that. Yasmine knew that complications were to be avoided whenever possible, and that men were attracted to her for one reason alone.

But she watched and listened as Kyle launched into conversation with her meddlesome friends, fielding their nosy questions and behaving like a relaxed boy-friend rather than a guy she was screwing for the week-end, and he almost convinced even her that they were an item.

"Where did you two meet?" Nora asked.

"We work in the same office."

"Ah, an office romance! I had no idea Yasmine worked with any cute guys. To hear her talk—"

"We're all a bunch of pasty-faced geeks."

"I'd hardly call you pasty-faced," she said, and Lio-nel cast her a look.

Kyle shrugged. "I do some surfing, get some fresh air now and then."

Across the room, Cass caught Yasmine's attention and waved her toward the kitchen. She slipped away from the group and followed her friend.

"What's up with you?" Yasmine asked as she sur-veyed the hors d'oeuvre tray Cass was preparing to take out to the crowd for something that didn't look burned.

"Try not to look too smug, but that guy Drew is what's up with me," Cass said as she tried to hide the burned spots on the finger foods with a layer of spray cheese.

"You like him!"

"Well, I can't say I didn't like him, but I don't know him well enough to know if I like him. What I do know is that there's definitely some chemistry going on."

Yasmine settled for an overdone mushroom and chewed it up fast to avoid experiencing too much of the flavor. "Let me just say for the record that the spray cheese isn't going to fool anyone."

"Aren't you going to comment on the chemistry thing?"

"I'll reserve my enthusiasm for your engagement announcement."

"Don't even go there."

"Okay, I'm glad you're giving Drew a chance. He's one of the nicest guys I know, and he deserves a good woman. So that means no stomping on his heart."

"Well, I can promise him some good sex, but that's about it."

She decided not to argue. Cass had been more into her ex-boyfriend than she had any other guy, and being dumped out of the blue had hit her hard. Even harder when the dumping happened over another woman. She was well past the rebound period though—it was time for her to move on to a guy who deserved her affection and get over her fixation on pretty, shallow men.

The acrid aftertaste of the mushroom hit Yasmine and she thought twice about bringing any of the cheese-sprayed mushrooms back to Kyle.

"I'd better go rescue Kyle," she said. "Soon as you've had your date with Drew, I want all the details."

"You've got a deal, so long as you give me a full report on Mr. Gorgeous out there."

"There's nothing to report. We're just being weekend sex buddies, I guess." She shrugged and turned away to avoid any further scrutiny.

Yasmine wandered into the living room, pausing near the doorway to watch Kyle interact with her friends. He was as relaxed as if he were among his own friends instead of a bunch of people eager to find out if he was his date's soul mate or if he had some monstrous flaw. And she marveled that for once, she didn't feel on edge introducing her date to her friends. She somehow felt just as relaxed as Kyle looked.

Bizarre, considering how little they knew each other, and how he could still reveal himself as an utter and complete nutcase, and she wouldn't have any right to act surprised.

In fact, any second now, Yasmine fully expected she'd wake up and realize Kyle Kramer wasn't nearly as great a guy as he seemed to be.

8

ALEX SIPPED his after-dinner eggnog and watched the lights twinkling on the Christmas tree. Around him, the ebb and flow of conversation lulled him into a half trance, the sort he remembered from his childhood that only came with being content and surrounded by family and friends.

He'd enjoyed hanging out with this group, talking over dinner and watching with detached amusement as half of them got into a heated debate over Trivial Pursuit. He was even having trouble remembering he was supposed to be someone else. Sure, there was the lying he'd had to do about his career, but he'd rehearsed that story so many times he'd almost started believing it.

And now, here with all Yasmine's friends, he felt as if he belonged, as if he was with a woman he really cared about and not one he was secretly trying to gather evidence against. It occurred to him, when he finally remembered his situation, that his life had gotten seriously screwed up.

Not only did he think Yasmine was the hottest thing since the discovery of fire, he was pretty sure he liked her just as well outside of bed. So far, she hadn't done a single thing to make him feel justified in secretly investigating her.

If she didn't start acting like an obnoxious criminal soon, he was going to develop a guilty conscience. Okay, who the hell was he kidding? He already felt guilty, and if he didn't find some solid evidence against her, he'd feel like the world's biggest jerk for ever having lied to her in the first place.

The Trivial Pursuit game ended with a resounding victory for the women—owed entirely to Yasmine's amazing wealth of useless knowledge—and she flopped down next to him on the sofa where he'd been sitting content to watch, not contributing much to the game.

"You're looking awfully contemplative. Ashamed that your team lost so badly?" she asked, her dark eyes sparkling.

"You know more than any normal human should about American history."

"Side effect of attending expensive boarding schools."

Which must have made going from a stimulating intellectual environment to a youth correctional facility an even bigger shock for her. He'd blocked out that fact before, but now, sitting here with her, he had a pang of empathy for the spoiled little genius girl who'd been locked away thanks in part to him.

"Did you get to wear hot little plaid skirts and white tops knotted at the waist?" he half whispered.

She laughed. "Yeah, and we dressed in little pink teddies on Saturday nights and had all-girl pillow fights."

"A guy can dream, right?"

"And you're also pretty good at evading questions. What's with the brooding expression you were wearing a minute ago?"

"Seriously? You want to know the truth?"

Yasmine leaned in close and propped her head on her elbow against the back of the sofa. "Absolutely."

"I *hate* eggnog. Why on earth do people drink this crap?" He gazed down into his cup as if worms were emerging from it.

She laughed and swatted his thigh. "You're a freak."

"Only in the bedroom."

Around them, people were donning coats, gathering purses and unwrapped gifts, saying goodbyes. Alex realized, out of the blue, that as much as he loved Yasmine's company, this was truly an awful way to celebrate Christmas Eve, spending it deceiving a woman he didn't want to deceive. He was so far removed from the spirit of the season that he might as well have donned a devil costume and called it Halloween.

"Let's go," Yasmine said, "before you do anything violent to your eggnog."

"Definitely."

The darkest, ugliest part of him had brought Alex to this point, and he realized now his mistake was in thinking that a good end justified dishonest means.

Five minutes later they'd said their goodbyes and were outside, walking back to Yasmine's apartment. She was tucked into his side, her hip bumping against him as they walked down the street.

"I hope my friends didn't drive you crazy," she said.

"They were great. I had fun tonight."

"Thanks for being my date—and for keeping me company over the holidays, too. You're still staying the night tonight, aren't you?"

"Truckloads of eggnog couldn't keep me away. And I'm the one who should be saying thanks."

"We'd better stop the lovefest before we make each other sick, don't you think?"

"I think if you show me any appreciation, it should be for sharing my piece of Yule log with you."

"Oh, right. My dear friend Cass is many things, but talented chef is not one of them. That Yule log tasted like—"

"Like something better used for kindling?"

Here he was again, nearly forgetting that Yasmine wasn't his girlfriend or even his date. She was a woman whose company he wasn't supposed to be enjoying, and damn if he could help himself.

Focus. He had to shove aside his feelings of pleasure, of guilt, and focus on the task at hand. Time to dive into his investigation headfirst. He couldn't change his plan now, regardless of how underhanded it might be. "It's great that you've moved on from your time in juvenile detention and built a new life for yourself. Your friends seem really nice."

"They are. I'm lucky I have people who don't judge me."

"Except when it comes to Trivial Pursuit."

She smiled, and he could sense her relaxation. "Right," she said. "I like them because they don't care what I can or can't do with a computer."

"Aren't you ever tempted to test out your hacking skills?" he asked, casual as he could be.

She sighed. "I'll admit, it's a temptation."

"I can imagine. I mean, honestly, I used to play around, trying to break into systems, but I sucked. I'd make a terrible hacker," he lied.

"Yeah, well, it's not exactly a skill to be proud of."

"Sure it is. I mean, assuming you were doing it for the right reasons." His stomach clenched. This was the point where he could ruin everything if he wasn't careful.

"Now there's a daring idea."

"What?"

"That it's okay to do something wrong if you've got a good reason."

"Sort of like Robin Hood. Stealing from the rich to give to the poor."

"You really believe Robin Hood was a good guy?" she asked, and Alex's heartbeat quickened.

He knew he was close. So damn close.

"Yeah, doesn't everybody?"

"Not the rich people he stole from."

He glanced over at her and caught her smiling. "Is there something you're not telling me?"

"Promise you can keep a secret?"

"Sure," he said as evenly as he could.

"Remember that story in the news a while back, about the hackers who were attacking terrorist Web sites?"

"Yeah," he said, a weird sense of anticipation settling over him. "That was great—why?"

She smiled, all mock innocence. "Well…"

"That was you?"

"Me and some friends. It was a blast."

Alex felt as if someone had clubbed him in the head. It made sense now. She had been hacking again, but perhaps not in the way he or any of his fellow agents had thought. At least in this case, not for any nefarious purpose.

Holy shit.

"You're kidding!"

"No, I'm not. But please keep it quiet, okay? I've

never told anyone, and…given my history, I don't want word getting out."

"My lips are sealed. But that's awesome. I mean, how many Web sites did you take down?"

"Between me and my friends, probably about twenty hits over a two-month period. That's counting repeats—when they got their sites back online, we took them out again." She smiled, and he could tell she was proud of herself even if she didn't want to admit it.

"What made you stop?"

"Guilt, and a weird feeling, like this sense I had that I was going to get caught again. I started feeling like I was being watched."

"Who would prosecute you for hindering terrorists?"

"I guess I'm just paranoid. I know it sounds crazy."

"Not at all." His chest filled with an odd sense of pride in her. In her own way, she'd been helping to defend her country.

"I've always felt—I mean, since the first time I got in trouble—like I had to walk the straight-and-narrow path or else. I just had this little impulse to do something rebellious, but then I got scared."

"Is that what this weekend with me is about? Being a little rebellious?"

"No," she said too quickly. "I mean…maybe, a little."

"I see," he said, smiling.

And now he understood his appeal to her. She was a rebel without an outlet for her urges, and he was her way to rebel. He was dangerous, but not too dangerous. It wasn't the way he'd intended to gain her trust, but it had worked nonetheless.

"You're not offended, are you?"

"Let's see—a beautiful, intelligent woman wants to spend the weekend with me. Which part should I be offended by?"

Yasmine shrugged and looked ahead as they walked. There was some shift in her mood then that he couldn't quite put his finger on.

And the question remained—had she engaged in any other system intrusions? Was she only telling him part of the truth? Was her daring to hack into terrorist Web sites just a hint of her secret activities?

Alex glanced at Yasmine again, her perfect features aglow in the streetlights. He couldn't fathom her, this rebellious beauty who'd captivated him from the moment he first saw her. And he hoped like hell that she was innocent.

But then what? What if she really was innocent? Did he think he could just tell her the truth and that they could continue as they'd started this weekend? No, he knew there would be repercussions, and no matter what he learned from his investigation, both of them were going to get hurt.

ALEX HAD SET HIS WRISTWATCH alarm to sound at two in the morning, and as soon as he heard it go off, he pressed the button to stop the tinkling alarm. Beside him, Yasmine slept soundly, her steady breathing marked by the occasional pauses of deep sleep.

He allowed his eyes to adjust to the dark, then lay in bed biding his time. He could get up right now and search her computer, search her apartment, look for any and all answers to the question of her involvement in illegal activities.

Part of him couldn't wait to know the truth, was eager to prove that she was innocent. And another part of him dreaded the other possibility—the chance that she really was still a hacker. If his attraction to her had clouded his judgment that badly, he wasn't sure he wanted to know that, either.

But he'd come this far. He'd concocted a false identity for himself, lied his way into Yasmine's life, and he couldn't back down now.

One more glance in her direction to confirm she was sleeping, and he slipped out of the bed, silent and easy. Grabbing his boxers from the floor, he slid them on and eased his way out of the room and into the living room, where the lights on the tree still twinkled.

Alex sat at the computer desk and with a nudge of the mouse, took the monitor out of low-power mode. Yasmine's flat-panel screen came to life, bright blue in the near darkness, inviting him to explore whatever secrets the hard drive held.

The type of people who spent their free time invading other people's systems tended to be a paranoid sort when it came to their own computer's security. Passwords and firewalls abounded, but Yasmine's system came to life without a single password request.

Without that hurdle to jump, he easily started exploring. Through folders hidden and not so hidden, he looked for clues about her Internet activities. That everything was so easily accessible was a good sign, a sign that she didn't think like a hacker anymore.

And after a half hour of poking around her hard drive, he'd have to say, if she had any secrets, they were hidden *extremely* well. On the Internet, she seemed to have a penchant for Ebay and online shopping sites, a couple of news sites and blogs, and that was it. Nothing nefarious. She didn't haunt any of the sites attractive to hackers, didn't even go to sites that suggested she might have an interest in system security anymore.

He breathed a sigh of relief.

His eyes glazed and his body telling him what he needed most was sleep right now, he glanced at the dark hallway that led to the bedroom.

No sound came from that direction, but something made his hackles rise. He went totally still and listened.

Nothing. Maybe it had just been the cat. But his muscles remained tense, his senses on alert, so he turned back to the monitor and set it to low power again.

When he was about to rise from the desk chair, an almost imperceptible sound caught his attention. He turned and saw Yasmine standing in the living room doorway squinting in the soft light, her long hair tousled, falling over her shoulders and breasts.

The fear of nearly getting caught shot through him, seized his chest, sent his brain scrambling for an explanation of his late-night visit to her computer desk. It occurred to him now how horrified he was at the thought of Yasmine finding out the truth about his deception. He didn't want her to know, regardless of her guilt or innocence. He didn't want her to hate him.

She was still naked, and if it weren't for the cold spike of adrenaline that now had him on edge, he would have gotten hard at the sight of her. Shielding her eyes from twinkling lights on the tree with one hand, she frowned at him.

"What are you doing?" she asked. "I heard a noise and thought Santa had come."

He forced himself to breathe. "I'm kind of an insomniac. Couldn't sleep, so I thought I'd get up and check the news on the Internet."

A slow smile spread across her lips as she closed the distance between them. "I thought I'd properly tired you out tonight."

Alex stood and took her in his arms, relaxed into the warmth of her body. Thank God she'd bought his story.

"Mmm." He dipped his head down and kissed her. "I may need a little more exercise before I'll be ready to sleep."

"Exercise? Is that what we're calling it now?" she asked, and then she placed a kiss on his neck that he felt all the way to his groin.

"Call it what you want," he said. "Whatever it is, it's addictive."

The swiveling computer chair was behind him now, and she molded her body tighter to his. He brushed her hair back off her shoulders to give him unobstructed access to her breasts, and his cock went hard, while his balls tightened.

"Do you think Santa will still come if we're awake and…exercising?"

He silenced her with a long, hungry kiss, forcing his tongue into her mouth, overwhelming any doubts she might have had about his intentions. She was what he wanted more than air, more than food, more than water. She had to know that by now—and yet she was the last thing he should have wanted.

"I guess you could say Santa's already here and about to give you his own special kind of holiday cheer."

"Ohh, bad Santa," she purred. "I can't wait to see what you've got for me."

"It's something every girl can use," he said as he urged her toward the bedroom.

But she held her ground. "No, let's do it here," she said. "On the desk?"

"It's sturdy." She tugged him toward the side of the desk, pushed aside a stack of papers and sat, while he grabbed a condom from the stash they'd left on the coffee table earlier.

Alex wedged himself between her bare legs as she tugged down his boxers. Then he slid on the condom. His attention, torn between his guilt over snooping on her computer and Yasmine's irresistible body, found its focus where their bodies met and generated maximum heat.

Alex pinned her on the desk, pressing his body into her, finding the point of least resistance and sliding in. She had such a sweet, hot pussy, and an incomprehensible ache built inside him as he began moving inside her, probing as deep as he could go, then withdrawing and probing again.

He rested his weight on his elbows and looked into her eyes, wanting to see what was really there. Some hint of the truth about Yasmine. But all he saw was their dark depths. She was, as always, secret, hidden away, unfathomable except when it came to her sexual desires.

And then he saw something else. She looked at him with such vulnerability, it transformed her into a girl instead of a woman.

"What's wrong?" she whispered.

He stilled. "You tell me."

She tightened herself around him. "You just seem kind of intense right now."

"This…" he said, easing deeper into her. "What we've been doing…it's getting intense."

No other way to describe the crazy, hot, burning, aching need that kept pushing them into each other's arms. It was intense like nothing else he'd ever known.

9

YASMINE PEERED out the kitchen window at the gray Christmas morning while she heated water for instant cocoa in the microwave. She recalled the feeling of being watched that she'd had in the past few months, and realized that having Kyle here with her had eliminated that paranoia. For the first time in a long time, she felt completely safe and at ease.

She mixed the cocoa in steaming hot water, poured it into two coffee mugs and was about to carry them into the bedroom to wake up Kyle with when a hand slipped around her waist, and she felt herself pulled back against the firm warmth of a large male body.

"Ho-ho-ho, Merry Christmas," Kyle said.

"Hey," she said, her heart racing at the surprise. "I almost spilled your cocoa."

"Sorry, I woke up and felt lonely to find myself in an empty bed."

"Ready to open presents?"

"Before breakfast?"

"It's Christmas morning!"

After returning home from the party, they'd wrapped up the cheap souvenirs they'd bought at Fisherman's Wharf and Pier 39 and put them all under the tree to keep things looking festive.

"Oh, right. And Santa might have brought me that new surfboard I told him about."

"Not if you've been bad." She elbowed him in the ribs, and he held her tighter, splaying his fingers across her belly.

"I don't know why he got so freaked when I sat on his lap," he said, and Yasmine smiled at the image of Kyle balancing on a disgruntled Santa's knees.

"Santas these days have too much attitude."

"That's not what you said last night."

"True, and now that you mention it, I happen to know for a fact that Santa was way too busy last night to be hauling a surfboard down my chimney."

"You don't even have a chimney."

"Santa's a nasty boy, always looking for some tight space to get into."

"I think you're the nasty one," he said as he swatted her on the backside.

"So I've been told. Now grab your coffee and get your ass over to the Christmas tree." She swatted him back as he turned toward the tree.

Chilly as it was in her drafty apartment, Yasmine couldn't very well let Kyle sit around in his boxers—today's pair covered with snowmen. They were festive, but they wouldn't do much to keep the chill out. She grabbed a couple of blankets from the closet and gave him one before wrapping the other around herself and settling in next to the tree.

"I call elf duty," she said as she grabbed the nearest gift.

"It's all yours, babe." He leaned back against the couch and sipped his coca, clearly enjoying himself more than he wanted to let on.

Yasmine had to admit, this was turning into the most fun weekend she'd had in a long time, Christmas or not. A few nights of great sex clearly had a positive effect on her mood, and she was just about as jolly as she could get.

She knew the gift she'd grabbed was for Kyle, but she made a show of examining the tag anyway. It was the box of See's Candies she'd gotten him before she knew anything about him but what a great ass he had. Only a few days ago, but it felt like a lifetime.

"For you," she said.

He unwrapped the package and withdrew the box of chocolates, then pried off the box lid.

"There's a companion gift for that."

He picked up a chocolate and bit into it. "Mmm, raspberry," he said. "My favorite."

Yasmine's grin must have been huge. "They're almost as good as sex, aren't they?"

He quirked an eyebrow. "I don't know about that. I mean, they're tasty and all—"

"I've always wondered if eating them during sex would heighten both experiences."

"We can test the theory out," he said.

"All in the name of science, of course."

"Because that must be the kind of thing scientific minds puzzle over."

"Of course." She handed him the box containing the furry handcuffs. "When they're not inventing life-saving gadgets like this."

"I get to open two in a row?"

"It's the companion gift."

He tore into the paper, then opened the white box and

pulled out the leopard-print handcuffs. "Ah, of course. Chocolates and handcuffs."

"I'll let you solve the riddle. Major bonus points if you do."

He narrowed his eyes at her. "Let me get this straight, you bought this stuff before you even knew we'd end up sleeping together...."

"To declare my intentions, of course."

"You planned to take advantage of me all along!" He was doing a really bad job of acting offended.

"Give it up, Bad Santa. It's not like I've stolen your virtue."

He twirled the handcuffs on one finger. "I'll need a demonstration of how these work later. Your turn to open something."

Yasmine recognized most of the boxes as things they'd wrapped last night, but one small box caught her eye. "What's this?" she said.

"Open it and find out."

It was unmistakably Kyle's wrapping job, with too much tape and uneven paper alignment. She tore off the packaging and found a box filled with a little stack of computer-generated coupons.

The top coupon read, "Good for one free sensual massage." She flipped to the next one, which read, "Good for doughnuts in bed." And the next one, "Good for unlimited fantasies fulfilled."

"Wow, I get to redeem these whenever I want?"

"Maybe not whenever. I mean, in the middle of the workday would be bad timing for most of them."

She smiled, touched that he'd taken the time to create a homemade gift. "Is this why you got up in the middle of the night?"

He shrugged. "Well, I couldn't sleep, and I felt bad for having woken you up."

"Didn't you ever see the episode of *Friends* when Joey gives coupons as gifts?"

"No, why?"

"Oh, nothing. Thank you," she said, and she meant it. "This is the sweetest gift anyone has given me in a long time."

She handed him his next gift.

"Is this one mine?" He made a big show of acting as if he had no idea what was in the package, even though he knew it was only the dumb key chain they'd bought yesterday.

"Wow," he said, holding it up for her to see. "It's in the shape of a cable car. Get it? Cable cars represent San Francisco."

She laughed. "You're such a dork. A cute dork, but still a dork."

They finished unwrapping their assortment of goofy little gifts and sat on the floor beside each other, drinking cocoa and playing with their stuff. Yasmine shook up her San Francisco snow globe and watched the glitter fall on the city.

"What's with you and the snow globe?"

She smiled. "I've got a collection of them. It used to drive my parents nuts that everywhere I traveled with them I could have picked out some tasteful, authentic souvenir—a piece of pottery or a local artist's sketch or whatever—and I always wanted a snow globe instead."

"Show me your collection sometime?"

"Absolutely!" She beamed. No one ever asked to see her snow globes.

"So, are you ready for that surfing lesson?" he asked.

"That what?"

"Didn't you see your last coupon? It's for a free surfing lesson."

"Only if you meant that in a figurative sense, like you're comparing surfing to sex again."

"No, I mean a real surfing lesson, with ocean and waves and wetsuits."

Yasmine looked at him as if he was speaking a foreign language. "I don't know why you think I'd want to do that."

"Because it's something new? Bet you've never gone to the beach on Christmas day before."

"As a matter of fact…no, I haven't, and I don't see any reason to break with tradition."

"Come on, this is the antitraditional Christmas celebration. You've got earrings hanging from your tree, we just exchanged sex coupons for gifts, and we've known each other for only a couple of weeks."

"And what does any of that have to do with surfing? Besides, I doubt any equipment rental places are open today."

"Doesn't matter. We can swing by my place on the way to the beach. I've got an extra board and a wet suit that'll fit you."

"Surf boards won't fit in my car."

"We can take my SUV."

"Jeez, you're persistent."

"Aren't you even a little bit curious about what it's like to ride a wave?"

"After all your sex and surfing metaphors, no. I think I've got a perfectly good idea, and I'm happy to stick with the sex side of the experience."

"Then come to the beach and watch me surf. Maybe next time you can try it."

Next time, as if they'd have more than just this weekend together. The idea intrigued Yasmine. There was nothing not to love about Kyle. Aside from his slightly furtive behavior that first night at his apartment, he was altogether a dream guy.

Finally, after years of dating guys who never saw past her appearance, she was starting to let herself believe that Kyle might be a real winner. It was a crazy idea, and totally unexpected, but what the hell. Kyle seemed to be genuinely interested in her.

So, yeah, maybe they would have more than just a weekend together. Maybe this thing that had started out as purely sexual would grow into something more.

"Okay, fine. I'll watch you surf, but if you freeze your private parts off, I have to tell you, you'll be of no further use to me."

He laughed and pulled her onto his lap. "Is that all I am to you—a sex toy?"

"Pretty much, yeah," she said, but her wide smile betrayed her.

ALEX STRETCHED OUT on the bed, enjoying the ache in his muscles from having spent the afternoon on his board. Yasmine had walked the beach, picking up shells, and by the time he'd finished surfing, she'd gathered a pocketful of perfect, unbroken shells that she'd insisted on showing him one by one now that they were back at her apartment.

She lined them up on the blanket. "Think I can make some kind of mermaid bikini out of these?"

"Hmm." He rolled over and grabbed two sand dollars. "Lie back and let me see if these fit you," he said as he held them up against her nipples.

She peered down at the shells. "They're a little small, huh?"

"Looks just right to me." He placed a seashell over her pubic hair, and she laughed.

"Unless I go for a full-frontal wax, that one's definitely too small."

"I don't know…." Seashells or no seashells, she looked amazing to him.

"Okay, no bikini." She scooped up the shells and put them on her nightstand, then lay back down beside him.

They'd stopped at a Turkish restaurant for dinner, and they'd planned to find a Christmas movie on TV to watch after returning to Yasmine's apartment, but instead they'd ended up in bed again.

Alex traced his fingers from the space between her breasts to her belly button, then made lazy circles around it. He loved the perfume she wore, something like spiced fruit, and he loved watching how she responded to his touch, her expression softening, turning dreamy.

He didn't want to spoil the moment, but now was as good a time as any to dig for information.

"Tell me about what you were like growing up," he said.

She laughed. "I'll spare you the boring details. I was a spoiled only child, my family traveled a lot, and that's about as interesting as it gets."

"Come on, those are just the facts. I mean, what were you *like?* Shy, extraverted, happy, sad, tomboyish, girly—that kind of thing."

"All of the above?"

"You're not going to make this easy, are you?"

"I hate talking about myself."

"Which clique did you belong to in high school?" he asked, moving dangerously close to the important topic.

She cast a crooked smile at him. "I was a computer geek, of course."

"I have a hard time seeing you as a geek."

"Well, maybe I wasn't the stereotypical awkward nerd in glasses and bad clothes, but I was bored in school and tended to do my own thing."

"Bored, as in you were too smart for your own good?"

"Something like that. I got into trouble, partly to entertain myself and partly to remind my parents I was alive." She covered her face and sighed. "See how boring this is? I'm just the typical spoiled little rich girl, desperate for my parents' attention."

"It's interesting to me. I don't think there's anything typical about you."

And that much was true. She fascinated him far more than he would have liked.

"What about you? Were you the homecoming king?"

He sighed. "No, I was actually kind of a skinny geek myself. I didn't really get into decent physical shape until college when I took up surfing."

"So which crowd were *you* in?"

"I thought I was the one asking the questions."

"I answered." She draped her bare leg over his as she turned onto her side, propping her head on her elbow and smiling. "But if you want every boring detail, we didn't have the traditional cliques most schools had. We had the rich girls and the really rich girls, the old-money girls and the new-money girls, that sort of thing. I'd like to say I rose above it all, but actually I mostly hung out in the rebellious crowd."

Now they were getting somewhere. Getting her to admit past offenses was a big step toward her admitting any more-recent ones.

"How much of a rebel were you?"

"Not that bad. Just kind of a petty criminal. Shoplifting and smoking cigarettes were my big rebellions, until I got hold of my first computer."

He shouldn't have felt sorry for her, but her expression reminded him of the girl she'd been, the girl who hadn't completely understood the consequences of her actions. She'd had to learn the hard way, and knowing her personally now, he felt bad that she couldn't have had an easier lesson.

"After you got out of juvenile detention, you were never tempted to…test out your skills any more?"

"God, no. Aside from what I told you last night, I've lived in complete fear of doing anything wrong again. I nearly screwed up my whole life, ruined what there was of my relationship with my parents and missed out on having a normal senior year of high school."

Another stab of guilt hit Alex. He'd never known he'd helped drive a wedge between Yasmine and her parents. Was there no damn end to the ways he'd negatively impacted her life? Sure, she'd been guilty of hacking, but some nagging voice inside him had always wondered if she'd deserved to be made an example by giving her the maximum sentence.

Hadn't he done enough?

He knew he had. He'd done more than enough. He shouldn't have insinuated himself in her life again.

What the hell was he doing here, besides trying to prove to himself that he wasn't inept as an investigator? Indulging his long-held desire for Yasmine? Was that what this was really all about?

He saw himself clearly for the first time, reflected in her gaze. He saw how low he'd sunk. His actions were not just underhanded, they were sleazy, despicable, unjustifiable...

And he couldn't go through with it anymore.

He'd already had more than enough of an impact on Yasmine's life, and he needed to stop before he did any more unintended damage.

Okay, admittedly, her stint in the juvenile detention center might have scared her straight, and if it really had, then he'd helped do some good in her life, too, but clearly, she'd paid a hefty price for her crimes.

Another problem remained. If he wasn't seducing her for information anymore—then where did that leave them, besides lying naked together in her bed on Christmas night?

"You're being awfully quiet," she teased. "Did I bore you to sleep?"

"No, I was just thinking it's sad you and your parents are so disconnected."

"Everybody's got their problems. Mine are pretty small in the great scheme of things."

"But still—"

"This is exactly why I didn't want to go into all this crap. I really didn't want you to feel sorry for me, or to think I'm damaged because I spent a year in juvie."

"I don't. I just hate that any of that stuff happened to you."

"I brought it on myself—end of subject," she said, smiling as she brushed her fingertips across his cock, her obvious and very effective attempt at distraction. "Now can't we think of something more interesting to talk about?"

His groin stirred at her touch, but he couldn't go there now.

"So long as it's not *my* dark and sordid past," he said, forcing his tone to remain light, joking.

"Do you need to call your family today?"

"Oh, right," he said. "It's still daytime in Hawaii, but I'd better call before long."

Yasmine had talked to her own parents this morning briefly, but Alex had put off calling, dreading thinking of what he'd say when they asked who he'd spent the holiday with.

Part of him wanted to flee the scene of his crime before he got caught.

And yet it was Christmas. He couldn't just abandon her, and he didn't want to. He wanted to stay and make love to her all night, all weekend, wanted to forget his real identity and become whatever man she imagined him to be. Clearly, he wanted too damn much.

He needed to tell her the truth, but now wasn't the time. He had to find the right time soon, though, before their emotions got any more complicated. Even at this level of intimacy, the fallout could be major.

"But seriously, stop joking around. I want to know all about you now."

"I'm the one with the boring past. Not much to tell."

Except that he was a lying, sneaky, good-for-nothing fraud.

"All I know about you is that you know how to survive in the wild, you surf, and that you started in college. Where'd you go to college?"

"William and Mary in Virginia. I grew up in Virginia Beach, went to school for a year at Old Dominion before I decided to make the switch to a school away from home."

"So you're a mama's boy?"

"Not exactly. I had to pay my own way through school, and living at home helped, but I got sick of it and decided to eat the cost of room and board."

"That's what student loans are for, right?"

"Exactly."

"So I guess between teaching survival skills and surfing, you've managed to stay a lot more fit that the average programmer."

"I have?"

"Haven't you noticed you're nearly the only guy in our office who doesn't have a paunch?"

Now there was a detail of his disguise he'd failed on. Not that packing on the pounds would have done much to help attract Yasmine's attention.

"Um, no. You're pretty much the only person at the office I've checked out."

"I'm flattered," she said as she brushed her fingertips along his bicep, sending chills through him. "I was just wondering, would this be a good time to start redeeming my coupons?"

His will to resist Yasmine lasted all of a nanosecond. "Absolutely."

10

"Unlimited sexual fantasies fulfilled?" Yasmine smiled at the little coupon and tried to imagine what she'd choose if she could have any fantasy come to life.

Aside from the fantasy she was already living—spending a weekend in bed with Kyle. Even now, lying next to him naked on her sofa, she felt as if the line between fantasy and reality had blurred, as if maybe this weekend wasn't really happening to her, but rather, she'd stepped outside of her own life and was living someone else's.

Kyle had just gotten off the phone with his parents, and she'd relished listening to his conversation. The way his voice softened a bit when he spoke to his mother, grew a little heartier as he talked to his father— it gave her a glimpse of what he was like as a son, and now, oddly, she was even more turned on by him.

She'd even been ridiculously flattered that he hadn't tried to hide what he was doing for the holiday weekend. He'd simply told his parents he was spending it with a female friend. No, they hadn't met her, and, yes, she was a lovely woman.

"Now there's a gift that keeps on giving. What fantasy would you like to have fulfilled today?" he asked as he rubbed his hand along her thigh and up her hip.

"Wow, I've never given this kind of thing much thought."

Kyle gave her a disbelieving look. "You work at a company that makes sex software, and you've never thought about your favorite fantasy?"

She shrugged. "I have lots of fantasies, but I don't really think about acting them out in real life."

The truth was, some of her favorite fantasies were kind of politically incorrect, and she couldn't imagine saying them out loud to anyone.

"Are you just too shy to admit what you want?"

"Me? Shy? Never," she lied.

"Maybe I should make one up for you then," he said.

"No! I mean, no, that's not necessary. I'll think of something…."

Maybe she needed to down some champagne, loosen herself up a little.

Or get over herself and ask for what she really wanted.

If there was any guy she wanted to act out her most secret fantasies with, she realized, it was Kyle. How had she come to trust him so quickly? She couldn't put her finger on any one reason. It was just a feeling, a sense she'd had since the first time they talked that they shared some familiarity, some past life that allowed them to pick up where they couldn't remember having left off.

"Well? What's it going to be? Me Tarzan, you Jane? We can act out the Jungle Honey game—how about that?"

She took a deep breath. Could she do it? Could she reveal a part of herself that she'd never revealed to any man? Yes, with Kyle, she could. She would.

"No jungle love right now. What I really want— I want to be tied up and taken…without my permission."

There it was, out there, hanging in the air between them.

"You mean, like I'm the thief, breaking into your bedroom, coming to steal your virtue?"

He didn't look altogether thrilled by the idea, although he didn't seem repulsed, either. Yasmine felt her face getting hotter and hotter.

"I know that's kind of weird. But," she paused and shrugged, "who ever said fantasies were realistic?"

"So tell me a little more about how you'd like this scenario to go."

"You could use the handcuffs. Maybe you didn't think anyone was home when you broke in, but now that you've found me..."

"And you're the lonely, neglected housewife, desperate for sexual satisfaction?"

"Mmm." She squirmed at his touch as he started tracing her breasts with his fingers. "Something like that. Of course, I'm not allowed to want you. But if you've cuffed me to the bed, what choice do I have but to lie back and enjoy the ride?"

She was getting hot at the thought of the scenario, and she wanted to do it now.

He smiled. "You get ready for bed, and I'll be going now—off to work. Be a good little wife while I'm gone, okay?"

Yasmine tried not to laugh. This was her fantasy, after all…. "Okay, honey." She gave him a chaste peck on the cheek, then stood up to go to the bedroom. "I'd better leave a window open tonight, it's so hot in here— sure hope no burglars are prowling around."

A few minutes later she'd put on a black lace teddy

and was standing at the dresser brushing her hair when the lights in the room went out, startling her a bit even though she knew what was going on. A moment later, rough hands clad in leather gloves grasped her and pulled her toward the bed. A thrill shot through her, leaving her a little breathless.

"Shh," he said. "No screaming. Cooperate and you won't get hurt."

She felt the handcuff clasped around one of her wrists, and then he pushed her onto the bed, pulled her to the center, and cuffed her to the iron headboard.

"My husband could come home any moment now. You'd better leave me alone," she said, not sounding very convincing, hoping her bad acting skills wouldn't ruin the fantasy.

"I'll leave you alone when I've had my fill of you," he said, raking his hands over her, under her teddy.

"No, please don't—"

He silenced her with a hungry kiss, and a hand pushed aside her panties. His leather-clad fingers rubbed her, forced their way inside her, where she was already slick and wet. She squirmed against him, pretending to struggle but loving every second of it.

Why did his domination of her feel so good? She didn't want to analyze it. Some things didn't need to be picked apart. Just enjoyed.

Then he was gone, and his absence left her feeling exposed and thrilled at the same time. She heard the sound of a condom wrapper, a zipper, and he was between her legs, pushing them wide apart.

"I'm going to taste you," he said. "Don't try to fight it."

"No."

She made an effort to move her legs, but he held them tight, and then his tongue was slick against her, dipping into her, massaging, coaxing her.

"Stop," she said between gasps of pleasure.

And then, to her dismay, he did.

"As you wish," he said, his voice hard-edged and taunting.

She whimpered and squirmed to no avail.

In the darkness, his shadowy form moved over her, but their bodies didn't touch as he lowered his mouth to her ear. When he drew her earlobe between his lips and sucked, gooseflesh dotted her skin.

"You want me, don't you?"

"No," she whispered. "Leave, please."

"If you want me to leave, why are you so wet?"

His gloved fingers again were between her legs, massaging her in a circular motion. Yasmine gasped, struck again by how fully she trusted this man who had complete control over her now. He could do whatever he wanted, and the danger of it thrilled her…yet she felt safe. He would never hurt her. She had so little frame of reference for that certainty, but she didn't doubt it for a moment.

She closed her eyes and gave herself over completely to the fantasy.

"Okay, you don't want to answer me? I'll just give you what you're afraid to ask for."

He grasped her hips as his cock found its destination.

"Bastard," she said.

Then he thrust hard into her, and she arched her back and cried out, having a difficult time pretending not to enjoy herself.

"You like this, don't you?" he said as he thrust again and again.

"Mmm," she moaned.

She wrapped her legs around his hips as he pounded into her, giving it to her hard and fast the way she wanted it. She loved that he knew what she wanted without her having to ask now. Loved the feel of him deep inside, stretching her, forcing her closer and closer to orgasm.

"You knew I was watching you through the window, didn't you?"

"Yes," she said. "I knew."

"You want me to make you come?"

"Yes," she cried out, and a few seconds later she was there.

Her legs locked around him, she felt something inside her give way as she gasped in the rush of her orgasm. Her body drinking him in, he came, too, his moans drowning out hers as he gave his final thrusts. Then they collapsed together, spent and breathless.

Yasmine nuzzled her face into him as they caught their breath, her mind reeling with the implications of what she might start to hope for in their relationship now. Now that she knew how deeply she trusted him, how different she was sure he was from the men who'd never seen past her surface.

A few minutes later he pulled away from her and freed her from the handcuffs. "Wow," he said. "Got any more fantasies you want acted out?"

"I think that's enough political incorrectness for one night," she said, smiling.

But clearly, she'd spent far too long ignoring her fantasy life.

"Just let me know," he said, spooning up against her on the bed. "I'm available for any and all requests."

"How about you?"

"The coupon is yours, not mine."

"Okay, then my next fantasy request is to fulfill your favorite fantasy."

"Hmm," he said. "That sounds like a twisting of the rules to me."

She laughed. "Guess I forgot to read the fine print. Now, come on, I told you mine. You tell me yours."

"In the spirit of political incorrectness, I have to admit…."

"Come on! Spill it."

"I've always had this thing for peep shows."

She bit her lip and smiled, rolling over to look him in the eyes. "You mean, like the ones where you pay a dollar and get to see a naked chick?"

"Something like that, though I'm guessing they cost more than a dollar these days."

"That might be kind of hard to duplicate," she said, giving the matter some thought. "But I do know a place…."

The strip club where Cass used to work had a little of everything when it came to X-rated entertainment, and Yasmine was pretty sure she'd heard Cass describe some private rooms that might fit the bill for a full-on peep show fantasy.

"Really, it's the element of voyeurism that's appealing. I like the idea of watching a woman put on a show—"

"But there's more to a peep show than voyeurism. It's a kind of seedy, dark, sex appeal. It requires the right setting and props to be effective."

"We don't have to make it so complicated. In fact, I've got plenty of other fantasies we could act out."

"No, this is the first one that came to mind, and I like it. I just need a little time to make some arrangements, find the right props, and your fantasy will be fulfilled."

"It's awfully generous of you to share your coupon with me."

"Purely for selfish reasons, trust me. In the meantime, I think I saw a massage coupon in my gift package...."

"Ready to redeem it?"

"Mmm-hmm." She rolled onto her belly and rested her head on her arms.

Kyle sat up and straddled her hips, removed his gloves, and dragged his fingers lightly up her back, sending tingling sensations through her. He started kneading her flesh, finding tense spots around her shoulder blades and neck and working them out, and Yasmine felt herself relaxing by a degree with each stroke.

In a matter of minutes, she'd be asleep if he kept it up. But he quickly moved on from her back to her arms, then her legs, then her feet. And after he'd finished working the kinks out of her feet, he moved up her legs again and slid his fingers inside her.

She hadn't been expecting it, and her breath caught in her throat. She arched her back and invited him in deeper, her body instantly heating at his touch.

"I've never had a massage like this before," she said.

"This is a little bonus I reserve for only my favorite clients."

He slipped one finger up and found her clit, while his other fingers remained inside her, working her until she must have been dripping wet. She moaned and squirmed, but he held her still, working his fingers around, in and out, then stretching her inner muscles as she began to contract around him. The sensation was incredible, and so close on the heels of her last orgasm, she came again with very little buildup.

When Kyle stretched out behind her and warmed her body with his, tucking her against him and holding her tight, she closed her eyes, started drifting off to sleep as the question formed her in head—could it get any better than this?

BECAUSE THE VIRTUALACTIVE offices were closed today, the day felt like any other Sunday, and Sunday mornings always evoked a sense of laziness in Yasmine. They made her want to curl up and read, go for long, meandering walks in the park and generally be unproductive. The Monday after Christmas, alone with Kyle, brought on those feelings twofold.

They'd spent the morning eating doughnuts in bed and working their way through the rest of Kyle's Christmas coupons—except for the surf lesson, which Yasmine ripped up and threw away the second time he suggested using it. By afternoon, it became clear that they'd have to leave the apartment to get a decent hot meal, so they reluctantly dressed and strolled down the street to an Italian dive for pizza.

But by the end of lunch, Yasmine was plagued with the thought that the sexfest had come to an end. Their little weekend of escapist fun was drawing to a close. The idea of work and a return to reality looming the next day had a lot to do with it, but also, it seemed as though something about Kyle had changed since last night.

He seemed more serious, a little morose, even. And she didn't have the guts to broach the subject.

Now, back in her apartment and lying on her bed stuffed full of pizza, staring up at the ceiling, Yasmine had the uncontrollable urge to brighten Kyle's mood with something silly.

She sat up and slid to the edge of the bed and down to the floor, then pulled an old box that had once contained a pair of purple suede boots out from under her bed. She climbed back up with it and sat down next to Kyle, then shot him a look meant to seem pregnant with importance.

"What's in there?" he asked, sitting up.

"The snow globe collection. I haven't shown it to anyone in years."

"Why not?"

"Because everyone thinks they're lame."

"Maybe everyone else is lame." The corner of his mouth twitched, and his tone was light again, as if the cold front that had descended was moving on.

Yasmine smiled as she lifted the dusty top off the box. "That's sweet, but you probably hate snow globes too."

"*Hate* is a strong word."

"You do hate them!"

"I like anything that makes you smile as much as that San Francisco snow globe did."

Each globe in the box was wrapped in tissue paper, and when she unwrapped the first one, she saw that it was from Istanbul. She shook it, and snow fell on the brilliant blue roof of the Aya Sofia.

"Now there's an event you don't see every day— snow on the blue mosque."

"I bought this one at a Sunday bazaar. I remember my mother and I were the only women there that day, and dressed in Western clothes no less."

"Were you freaked out?"

"I thought it was a great adventure. It never occurred to me to be freaked out."

She handed the small plastic globe to him and took out the next one. It was from Paris. Inside the globe, a tiny replica of the city's most famous attractions stood unnaturally close to each other. The Eiffel tower next to Nôtre Dame, which was only a fraction of a space from the Louvre, which sat just below the hilltop Sacre Coeur. Yasmine turned it upside down, then right side up again, and snow fell on the plastic tourist attractions.

"Ah, Paris," Kyle said.

"Have you ever been?"

"Once, on a whirlwind tour of Europe during college. I don't remember much."

"Oh, come on, how could you forget anything about Paris?"

He smiled. "Okay, I remember lots of pretty, well-dressed women. And a long line at the Eiffel tower. How's that?"

"Just like a man."

He took the snow globe and shook it himself. "How so?" he asked, playing dumb.

"You go to one of the most romantic, unforgettable cities in the world and don't notice most of it because you're too busy staring at the women." She tried to look offended, but really, it was just so typical, she could hardly find offense.

He shrugged. "Hey, I was twenty, and it was a quick

visit. I tried to focus on the important stuff. What can I say?"

She grabbed a green beaded pillow from the bed and walloped him with it.

"Ouch, those beads sting."

He put the Paris globe away, and Yasmine took out another one, unwrapped it, and smiled at the gaudy little London scene, a souvenir she'd bought from a sidewalk vendor. When she looked up at him, she caught that serious look again.

"What's wrong?"

"Other than the physical abuse?" He smiled, but it looked forced this time.

"You've been in a mood ever since lunch."

"I guess I just hate to see the weekend end, you know?"

Did she ever. "Me, too. I feel like we've been on vacation from life or something."

"We have been. I've done stuff this weekend I haven't done at all since moving to San Francisco. Next stop, Alcatraz."

"We'll save that for another weekend," she said before catching herself.

Would there be another weekend? Could there be? Did either of them really want it? She tried to imagine again letting their weekend fling turn into a relationship and invade their real lives, and butterflies stirred in her belly.

Kyle gave her a look that was both warm and curious. "Are you okay with going back to work tomorrow?"

"I don't know. Are you?"

"It's going to be a little odd. I mean, since we decided at the outset that we'd keep this out of the office—"

"Right, and we should."

Why couldn't she just tell Kyle she was falling for him? Why couldn't she get past her fears? But she of all people should have known that taking things too far could lead to disaster. This weekend fling was a lot like her short-lived reentry into the world of hacking when she'd helped take down terrorist Web sites. It had given her a thrill, and then she'd kept her control. She'd walked away.

Her gut told her walking away from Kyle was the right thing to do, too. The safe thing to do.

Her inner wild child longed to invite him to stay the night again, but instead she put away her snow globe collection and suggested she had laundry to do to get ready for work.

Kyle glanced at his watch. "Oh, yeah," he said. "Guess I should be heading home and doing the same."

Yasmine stood up from the bed and he followed her. She tried to think of something to say but couldn't.

Kyle took her hand and pulled her close. "I'll see you tomorrow at work, okay?"

"Okay, but—"

"We won't mention this weekend." His expression turned serious.

Yasmine sighed. "Right. I'll give you a ride home."

She placed a kiss on his cheek, which seemed ridiculous given their recent intimacy, but suddenly she felt stiff and standoffish. He quickly gathered his things, and they headed out the door, which should have been a relief for Yasmine.

But they rode back to his place in an uncomfortable silence, all the things they should have said but didn't hanging between them. In front of Kyle's apartment, they said an awkward goodbye, and Yasmine drove home feeling utterly confused, torn by the conflicting ideas that this weekend had either been the most exciting thing she'd done in a long time or a huge mistake.

Or both.

The moment she was alone in her apartment, her feelings of paranoia and loneliness returned with a vengeance. She'd made a mistake sending Kyle away so brusquely. And she couldn't stop thinking about him. Couldn't stop thinking about the whole idea of fantasy fulfillment, and how much she wanted to do for him what he'd done for her. So after she'd started the laundry and cleaned up her apartment, she picked up the phone and called Cass.

"How's Mr. Wonderful?" Cass asked when she heard Yasmine's voice.

"He's gone home now, but we had a rather steamy Christmas together."

"I could tell. There were major sex vibes in the air the other night between you two."

"There were not!"

"Please. You looked at each other like you were starving."

"That could have been because of your cooking, you know."

"Oh, you did not just go there."

"Sorry. Really, thank you so much for having us over, and in the future, please don't feel like it would be rude to order pizza delivery." Yasmine laughed, only because she knew Cass could make fun of herself.

"Please come get this damn *bûche de Noël*. Even the homeless guy on my block won't eat it."

"You should be ashamed of yourself, trying to foist that thing off on the less fortunate."

"I know. I bought him a new pair of shoes to make up for the offense."

"I hope you can extend that sense of generosity to a less-needy person in your life. Namely me. I need a favor," Yasmine said.

"Oh? After you insulted my cooking?"

"I'm truly sorry. Now do you think you could hook me up with a private peep show room at the Pink Pussycat?"

"Whoa, mama. Back up there for a sec."

She could almost see Cass's perplexed look over the phone.

"I owe Kyle a little fantasy experience, okay? I need a peep show room to do it, and I was hoping you could talk to the manager at the club, pull a few strings… I'm willing to pay, of course."

"So you need a room, but not a girl."

"Of course no girl—*I'm* the girl in the fantasy!"

"Hey. You never know how many girls might appear in a guy's fantasy."

"True, but I'm not down with that."

"I'll see what I can do. When do you need the room?"

"Um… I was kind of hoping for today."

"I'll call you back," Cass said.

"Thank you, thank you, thank you."

"Don't thank me yet. Wait until I get you what you want to grovel at my feet."

Yasmine hung up the phone and sat at the computer, then opened her e-mail program. She downloaded her e-mail and smiled when she saw a message from Kyle among the junk mail, right below a spam e-mail with the subject header:

Impress Your Girl with a Huge Cum Shot.

Okay.

She'd only dropped him off at his place an hour ago, so the fact that he'd already written her was totally intriguing.

The subject line read, "Forgot to say..." and when she opened the message, her smile grew.

I'm looking forward to seeing you tomorrow. Does midnight count as tomorrow? If you're reading this before bed, do you mind if I stop back by? I don't think I can wait until daybreak to see you.

By the time stamp on the message, she could tell he'd sent it about ten minutes ago, so she hit reply and typed:

Are you still online?

She got a little thrill when her program chimed notification of new mail in her inbox a few seconds later. Closing her Web browser, she saw a reply from Kyle waiting for her.

Yes, I'm here. Meet me in IRC?

He listed the URL of a private Internet relay chat room, and Yasmine followed the link he'd sent to the room.

There she found Dark Horse waiting for her. She typed:

What's with the name?

I'm in a dark mood.

What's wrong?

All this distance.

I don't get it.

You. Me. Too much distance between us.

Yasmine smiled, a little chill skittering over her at the thought of Kyle already missing her. She typed:

So come back over.

Wouldn't that seem a little odd?

To who? Me? You?

Yeah.

I don't think you need to worry.

Maybe we should be practicing restraint.

She laughed and typed:

Re-*what*? I'm not familiar with that word.

I noticed. Not that I'm complaining or anything.

You like my lack of restraint?

I'm a heterosexual male. I love your lack of restraint.

So what's the problem?

I need to get some actual sleep tonight, or my ass is going to be dragging tomorrow.

Me, too. We're a bad influence on each other.

How about we take care of our little problem right here. Online?

Yasmine was definitely liking the sound of a little on-line sex relief, but the phone rang. She typed:

Hold on a sec. Got a phone call.

She picked it up.

"I arranged a room for you," Cass said without introduction. "And you can have it right now if you want."

"Oh, thank you, thank you, Cass! I owe you for this."

"You'd better believe you do. Meet me for Pilates on Thursday?"

"Do I really owe you that much?" Yasmine said, wincing at the idea of rolling and crunching herself into muscle cramps.

"Yes, you do. When you arrive at the club, just go in the front door, head for the back, take a left in the hallway and go into room number nine. From there, you can ask around if you need help with anything else."

"I'll talk to you soon," Yasmine said before she hung up the phone again.

Turning her attention back to the computer, she typed:

I've got a better idea. Can I swing by and pick you up in fifteen minutes?

11

"I HAVE A SURPRISE for you," Yasmine said as she killed the car engine.

Alex peered out the passenger window and a saw that they'd stopped in front of the Pink Pussycat, an upscale strip club that catered to men with money to burn. Surely not their final destination. This just happened to be where she could find parking.

"What did I do to deserve a surprise?"

"You fulfilled my fantasy, remember? Now I want to fulfill yours."

"But...how—"

She leaned over the emergency brake and kissed him, ending his question. "Don't ask how. I've got connections."

He cast a glance at the Pink Pussycat again. "You mean, we're going in there?"

"They've got peep show rooms."

For once, Alex found himself stunned speechless. He'd told her about his peep show fantasy on a lark. It was something he'd never told anyone and something he'd never imagined actually doing.

"We really don't need to do this, you know. Some fantasies aren't meant to be acted out."

"Hush," she said. "Just get out of the car."

She got out, and Alex followed suit, trying to imagine just what she had planned. He walked with her to the entrance of the club and followed her inside, where dark corridors were lit with blue lights. After following a velvet-roped walkway, they emerged in the main club.

A large, U-shaped bar dominated one side of the club, and a stage dominated the other side. Dance music blared from speakers overhead, and on stage, a lone blonde did a pole dance for an audience of eight or ten guys.

He watched Yasmine's gaze slide over the whole scene without reacting. While he, on the other hand, found his natural guy instincts having a hard time looking away from the near-naked female in the room. He forced himself to keep his eyes on Yasmine.

She flashed a mysterious smile and took his hand. "I think the peep show is this way," she said as she led him toward the back of the club.

God help him. This woman, this setting, this crazy weekend—he was pretty sure the rest of his life was going to be damn dull in comparison. But he followed Yasmine anyway. If this was going to be the most exciting weekend of his life, he might as well take full advantage, peep show and all.

Yasmine stopped at a door bearing a sign that read Private and opened it. "Have a seat in here," she said.

"Where are you going?"

"I'll be in soon. No more questions." Her eyes full of mischief, Alex felt himself growing hard in his pants. So damn predictable.

"Okay, but hurry," he said as she urged him inside the small room and closed the door.

Alone, he found himself with a comfortable recliner chair, a side table bearing a drink, and nothing else. He sat and saw the sliding panel on the wall, right at his viewing level. For a peep show. His erection grew. He leaned back in his chair and picked up the perspiring glass of amber liquid.

A sip confirmed that it was whiskey and Coke, and he tried to focus on the burning sweet taste of it, tried not think too much about what may or may not be about to happen on the other side of the peep show panel. Yasmine had been full of surprises, and today was no exception. But he didn't want to get his hopes up, or imagine the wrong thing, or…

He heard footsteps on the other side of the panel, and he set the drink aside, then leaned forward, resting his elbows on his knees. The position put him inches from the peep show panel. A sultry dance song began to play over the speakers, and the panel slid open.

He peered through and saw a woman dancing, rocking her hips to the beat. It only took a second for his brain to register that the woman was Yasmine.

Her arms lifted overhead, she moved her hips back and forth, around and around, in a dance that was blatantly erotic without being raunchy. She wore a black latex bra and panties, with thigh-high black boots, and she didn't look at him. Rather, she danced as if no one was there, as if no one was watching.

She twirled slowly around, giving him a view of her firm, perfect ass clad in thong panties, and the air left his lungs. He reminded himself to breathe—in, out, in, out.

Sweet heaven, she was hot.

Yasmine trailed her hands down her torso as she

danced, then up again, cupping her breasts, lingering over her nipples, and then slowly unclasping her bra in front. When it fell down over her shoulders, she let it drop to the floor, then continued to fondle her breasts without the hindrance of fabric.

Alex's cock strained against his pants, and he wondered if it was acceptable to jack off in a situation like this. Or was he supposed to wait until she'd finished her dance and came to him?

When she pushed her breasts up and together, then dipped her head and licked herself, first one nipple, then the other, he didn't have any will left to hold out. He unfastened his pants in a hurry and started stroking his cock.

Abandoning her breasts, she slid her hands back down her torso, and as her hips gyrated, she hooked her thumbs in the sides of her panties and slid them slowly down her hips, turning as she did so. She bent over, giving him a full view of her pussy, and stepped out of the panties, then kicked them aside.

Another gyrating turn put her face forward again, and still, she made no eye contact with him. She seemed totally into herself, into the dance, completely focused on her own body, and the effect was seriously hot. He slowed the stroking of his cock to keep from coming too soon, and watched enthralled as she dipped her fingers between her legs and started stroking herself.

Oh, hell. He wanted her like crazy.

He'd broken out in a sweat. Could feel it dripping down the insides of his arms, felt it on his brow and upper lip. His entire body was heating up, tensing, overcome with that same trembling desire he'd come to associate with Yasmine.

Still stroking herself, she spread her legs and started working her way downward into a squat, ending with her legs spread wide in front of the peep show panel. She reclined on one arm and continued to stroke. Alex's mouth went dry as he watched her fingers glide between her lips, inside her opening, out again, in again.

She was moaning now, her eyes closed, her show completely convincing, outrageously erotic. The music changed from the midtempo dance beat to something slower, and he couldn't take it anymore.

"Get your hot little ass in here," he said.

She opened her eyes and looked at him for the first time. Stopped stroking herself and leaned forward. "No talking allowed," she said in a breathy little voice.

"This was fun and all, but I'm going to come in my pants if you don't get over here, and I'd much rather come in you."

"I'm sorry, sir. We're not allowed to interact with the customers." She gave him a look that was pure steam. "Now please, sit back and enjoy the show."

From somewhere he couldn't see, she produced a shiny black dildo. Crawling back away from the window again, she held the dildo to her mouth and licked it the same way she'd licked him, and, on her knees now, her legs spread wide, she gyrated her body slowly to the beat as she brought the dildo down between her legs and stroked it against her clit.

Alex's breath grew quick and shallow, and he all but abandoned his own pleasure as he found his attention completely focused on watching hers. Her eyes were closed again, her face softened with pleasure, her mouth open as she moaned and gasped. When she pushed the dildo inside herself, he nearly came.

A few more strokes, and he'd be there. But he couldn't. Couldn't miss a second of this show. She moved the rubber cock inside herself, clearly lost in her own pleasure, seemingly oblivious to the sweet, delicious pain she was causing him.

And then she brought it back out, caressing her breast with one hand and stroking the dildo against her clit with the other, rocking her hips against it, gasping hard…. He could see the tension building in her body, could see the moment before her release, so when she gave that final cry of pleasure, he knew it as if it were his own body.

Wanted to be there as if it were his own body. Felt weak and spent as if it was him and not her.

She recovered, and for the second time, made eye contact with him. She crawled to the small window. "I hope you enjoyed the show," she said in that same sex-kitten voice, right before shutting the panel in his face.

Alex looked down at his forlorn cock resting outside his pants. Surely she didn't mean to leave him hanging. That definitely wasn't part of the fantasy.

But just in case, he eased his boxers and pants back over his erection and did his best to zip up. Suddenly the small black room with the dim lights appeared to him as the airless box it was, and he wondered if he was supposed to leave now or stay put.

Unsure, hot and frustrated, he downed his drink in a few swallows and then rubbed the damp glass over his forehead to cool himself off.

A second later the door opened, and Yasmine stepped

in and closed it behind her. She was wearing a white robe and the black boots, and when she let the robe fall open, he saw that she was still naked beneath it.

He opened his mouth to commend her performance, but she shushed him before he could get a word out.

"I'm not supposed to consort with the customers." Still with the sex kitten voice. "But this once, I can make an exception."

She shrugged off the robe and crossed the small space between them, then swiveled the recliner so that it faced away from the wall. Then she bent down and tugged the lever on the side of the chair so that it reclined all the way. That done, she climbed on and straddled him.

"There's an extra charge for…personal services," she said as she unzipped his pants and took out his cock.

"Whatever it is, I'll pay it."

He saw now that she held a condom packet in her hand. She opened it and slid the rubber on him. "What sort of services would you like?"

This was so much hotter than his fantasy, so much better than what he could have imagined, he couldn't think of anything but burying himself inside her at that moment.

"I want to be inside you."

She mounted his cock. Since she was already wet from her own orgasm, he slid inside her with no resistance, and he expelled a pent-up sigh. Silently she began riding him, her movements slow and deliberate, her gaze locked on him.

With her breasts so close to his mouth, he couldn't resist tasting them, couldn't resist squeezing them together and relishing their soft fullness against his hands, against his tongue. "Is that allowed?" he asked belatedly, enjoying their game more than he ever would have suspected.

"There will be an extra charge," she said. "You kiss, you pay."

"Can I touch you?"

"Yes," she said, and he slid his hands over her torso, around her hips, to her ass.

He pressed her harder against him, coaxed her into a faster pace as the sweet tension mounted inside him. A few more strokes was all it would take, but he wanted her there with him, wanted to give her a little bonus for the hottest sex show he'd ever seen.

Slipping his fingers down, he caressed the cleft of her ass, dipped his fingers in, found her most sensitive spot and massaged her there. She gasped and ground against him, contracted around his cock, almost with him... A little more, and she'd be there... He pushed farther, flexed inside her, tried hard to hold himself back until just the right moment....

She came hard, bucked against him, cried out, and he let himself go, too. Just the way he'd wanted it. He spilled himself, felt the pure, white-hot release shooting out of him again and again, his cries mingling with hers until she collapsed against him.

He could feel her heartbeat, listened to their breathing, which slowed to normal again as minutes passed, and finally she stirred. She sat up and looked at him curiously.

"Merry Christmas," she said. "It's a little late, but I hope you liked it."

"Thank you," he whispered, unable to summon the

energy for full-on speech. "That's the sexiest present I've ever had."

The sexiest, the hottest, the most addictive. How he would ever convince himself to stop wanting Yasmine, he didn't have a clue.

CASS HAD NEVER DONE IT with a nerd. And now, on her way home from a perfectly wonderful dinner with Drew, she was torn between her physical desires and her more practical ones.

Decked out in her new baby-blue Christmas sweater, black leather skirt and matching knee-high boots, she'd dressed to get laid tonight, and, judging by the way Drew had stared at her throughout dinner, she was well on her way to achieving her goal.

But…

But what? She'd be a fool to let her unexpected fascination with Drew spoil her otherwise happy life. She'd finally figured out that she didn't really want or need a man in her life, hadn't she? She'd come to terms with her own unconventional desires, and now this? It was stupid. If she was as smart as she claimed to be, she'd take care of her physical urges and send Drew on his way before he caused any disruptions— before the inevitable crappiness that went along with every romantic relationship worked its way back into her life.

When Drew's car stopped in front of her apartment, she knew without a doubt she wanted to invite him up and find out what nerd sex was all about. All night long, she'd been surprised by the way her expectations of him and reality failed to match up. She'd found him endearingly sweet and genuine and interesting to talk to—none of which helped with her plan to remain single and happy.

Here she was bucking the normal female response again. Wasn't she supposed to be thrilled when she found a guy she really enjoyed being around? Wasn't this cause for celebration rather than angst?

She'd been with all sorts of men, but different as they'd been—some lone wolfs, some party guys, some charismatic leaders—they had all shared the one indefinable quality that equaled coolness. Drew, cute and nice as he was, did not possess that quality.

And something about his unapologetic geekiness fascinated her in a way she never could have anticipated.

She'd lost her mind.

Drew cleared his throat and turned to her. "So…"

"So," she repeated, gazing across the darkened car at him.

"I had a really great time tonight."

"Me, too."

"I'd like to see you again," he said, and Cass's mouth went dry.

She wanted to see him again, too. She did, but she didn't. She didn't want complications, she just wanted sex. Didn't she?

Of course she did.

"Come up for dessert," she said, taking the straightforward approach.

"Don't you have to work tomorrow?"

"Yeah, so?"

"I do, too. I've got an eight o'clock meeting," he said, glancing at his watch.

"Are you saying you don't want to come up?"

"No, I want to, I just—"

It's just that he really was so endearingly clueless about women, he couldn't figure out when he was being propositioned for sex.

"Worried about feeling a little sleepy in the morning? Drink some coffee."

He smiled then, a crooked, unrehearsed smile that she found charming. "Okay, I guess I can stay awhile."

Seriously, she needed to get laid. *ASAP.*

She needed some hot, sweaty sex to clear her head and remind her of the sole way men had proven useful in her life.

He got out of the car and came over to Cass's side to let her out, then escorted her up the sidewalk as properly as if they weren't about to get it on.

All night, he hadn't dared to make the slightest overt move on her. His restraint was charming in a 1950s sort of way. Definitely another first for Cass, who was a magnet for dogs of all kinds.

"Want some coffee?" she asked as she let him in the door.

"You have decaf?"

"No."

"I'd better not then. I get jittery."

"How about some warm milk?" She flicked on the hallway light, then the kitchen light.

"Are you making fun of me?"

"Possibly. But you're such an easy target, I should stop."

He gave her a look she couldn't decipher, and she decided she'd better quit being a smart-ass.

Having proven herself on Christmas Eve completely inept at using the kitchen for its original intended purpose, she saw no reason not to find a new use for the space.

"Are you a dessert man?"

"I can be tempted by the right thing," he said, his breath tickling her cheek. "I like pie."

"What kind of pie?"

"Cherry's my favorite."

She leaned in and placed a kiss on the side of his neck, then pulled back. "No cherries here."

"What do you have?" he asked as his gaze traveled between her eyes and her mouth.

"Some leftover sweet potato pie, but I made it, so it tastes kind of awful."

"I've tasted your cooking—it's not bad."

"You've tasted my finger. My dinner party, however, was a disaster. I burned almost everything except the stuff that didn't need to be cooked, and that stuff I managed to screw up in other ways."

"Some women's talents are best revealed outside the kitchen." He ran his finger along the neckline of her sweater, then down and around the outside of her breast, sending a chill through her.

"I've got talents that can be demonstrated in the kitchen—just not the traditional kind," she said as she edged her hand up his inner thigh, stopping just short of his crotch.

"Care to show me?"

"I was hoping to serve you something sweet, though. I did invite you for dessert, after all." She bit her lip, trying to think of anything she had in the apartment that wasn't burned or stale.

"I thought that was just your excuse to get me up here and have your way with me," he said, smiling.

"It was both, but I don't like to make empty promises."

"I'll forgive you."

"I've got some flavored coffee syrups. You can at least have something sweet in your coffee."

"I like my coffee straight, no frou-frou stuff."

"Me too. The syrups were a Christmas gift…. But maybe we could find some other use for them."

"What kind of use do you have in mind?"

"Definitely not what the manufacturer intended."

"Sounds like my kind of dessert."

Was she really have this conversation with this man? This man who'd spent the evening making her mostly forget to have an attitude? This man whose atrocious fashion sense and inability to dance hadn't done a thing to dampen her desire for him?

She needed to stay focused, keep her mind on the fact that this was sex for sex's sake, not getting-to-know-you sex, or let's-be-intimate sex, or promise-of-something-more sex. It was just plain, opportunistic sex.

"Wait a second," she said, then went in search of the box she'd gotten.

In the pantry, there it sat with a bow still stuck on it, a gift box of four flavored syrups. She grabbed it and tore open the packaging, then placed each bottle on the counter next to Drew.

"French vanilla, mint chocolate, hazelnut and raspberry. Which one do you want to try first."

"Honestly, I don't want any coffee."

"I don't mean in coffee. I mean, try on me."

"Try on you?"

"On me," she said, tugging her sweater over her head, getting down to business before he could do anything else sweet and disarming.

Underneath her sweater, she wore a purple-and-black lace bra that she absolutely was not going to taint with flavored syrup. She reached behind her back and unfastened the clasp, then let the bra fall to the floor.

Drew's gaze was fixed on her bare chest now, his mouth slightly agape. "I'm sure you taste fine without syrup," he said, sounding distracted.

"I do, but that's beside the point." She unzipped her skirt and slid it down her hips, taking her time, wriggling around enough to put on a proper strip show.

Now there were just her boots and her panties, which had matched her bra but which were also pointless in the face of flavored syrups. She hooked her thumbs on each side and slowly tugged them off an inch at a time. The boots could stay. They might not have been practical, but they were great for effect.

Drew's gaze had dropped lower, was pinned now on the apex of her legs. "You've got an amazing body," he said.

He was being overly generous. She had an okay body and a better-than-average sense of self-confidence. She'd learned long ago that men could be pretty well impressed by any woman who stood tall and acted proud of what she had, regardless of her imperfections. And one of the most important things stripping had taught her, surprisingly, was that self-confidence was the sexiest attribute a woman could have.

"Thanks," she said, going for the bottle of raspberry syrup.

She unscrewed the top and climbed up on the

counter, then straddled Drew, who was sitting on a bar stool. When her breasts were mere inches from his mouth, she tilted the syrup bottle over them and let the liquid drip onto one nipple, then the other.

A whoosh of breath expelled from Drew's chest. "Damn it, woman…"

It was the first time she'd heard him use profanity.

"You don't like raspberry?"

"I love it," he whispered, then took one of her nipples into his mouth and began to suck.

Warm fuzzies spread from her breasts to her crotch, as Drew's hands traveled up her inner thighs. Say what you wanted about his fashion sense, but the man had a way with his hands. His touch, so appreciative and undemanding, left her feeling like a sex goddess, like a woman made for pleasure.

He licked the syrup from her breasts, then moved his kiss to her mouth, standing up from the bar stool and sending it crashing to the floor behind him. He tasted like hot, sweet raspberries, and Cass, with all her smart-ass attitude, couldn't think of any place she'd rather be than in his arms right then, syrupy sweet as it was.

He pulled her against him and pressed his erection between her legs, rocking his hips lightly and stimulating her where it counted.

"Are you sure you want to do this?" he asked, all tenderness and retro charm again.

She realized then that Drew wasn't really an all-out nerd so much as he was a brainy, old-fashioned guy. But old-fashioned guys needed to get laid, too, right?

"Of course I'm sure. You have protection?"

"Yeah," he said, then pulled out his wallet and produced a condom. They'd probably need more than one, but she had a stash in her bathroom for later.

His glasses were all steamed up. "Can you see without these?" she said as she removed them.

"Everything's a little blurry."

Good, then he wouldn't notice the tiny flaws that continued to appear on her body the older she got and the longer she spent away from the stage. She set his glasses aside and started unbuttoning his shirt.

He had a nice chest, smooth and kind of firm, with flat pink nipples, and his belly, while it was certainly no six-pack, had its own masculine appeal. There was no way to explain what was so damn attractive about Drew, and she'd be interested to see if she was still as hot for him after they got it on as she was now. Was his appeal hormone-induced or lasting?

It didn't really matter, though. Because she had to remember, this was sex for sex's sake.

She opened the fly of his pants and pushed aside his briefs—tighty whities, just as she would have guessed— to find his hard cock waiting for her. Now here was a part of Drew no woman could argue the appeal of. He was thick and long, more than enough to satisfy.

She sheathed him with a condom, and he eased himself into her one delicious inch at a time. Slowly at first, they found their rhythm, locked together, taking their time tasting and kissing.

This was just sex, just sex, just sex, she tried to tell herself, but there was no denying how it really felt. No denying that some kind of magic was happening between them.

For the first time in years, Cass felt as though she was

being made love to, as though the joining of their bodies was for some other purpose besides an orgasm or two.

And all that unexpected tenderness made her even hotter, so that when he was finally moving frantically in her with their destination in sight, she was right there with him, overcome with too many emotions to name.

He leaned her back on the counter, and bottles of syrup toppled over, rolling off the countertop and shattering on the floor. The uncapped raspberry syrup bottle spilled and created a sticky sweet pool near Cass's left shoulder, and moments later, when she came, bucking hard against him, she didn't give a damn that her hair got stuck in the mess.

Drew silenced her cries with a long, soft kiss that ended in his own orgasm. And his breath, his moans, were muffled in her hair until he stilled moments later and looked her in the eyes.

"You're incredible," he whispered.

"So are you," she said.

For once, it wasn't just pillow talk—or counter talk, in this case. She meant it.

But damn, why couldn't he have been ordinary or dull or a total asshole? Why was it that when she'd finally found true happiness, the universe decided to hand her the one thing she'd been absolutely sure she didn't want?

12

ALEX UNDERSTOOD, all too clearly now, that he was a weak, undisciplined man. It was no wonder he hadn't lasted in the FBI. Put his greatest sexual temptation in front of him, and he couldn't think of anything else, couldn't tear his attention away from her.

It was Tuesday afternoon, and his first day's attempt at pretending he and Yasmine had never happened had been a sad one so far at best.

He peered over the wall of his cubicle and spotted Yasmine across the room. Even the top of her head as she leaned over someone's computer turned him on. A thousand swimsuit models couldn't have had the same effect on him that she'd had this weekend, that she continued to have even now when he was supposed to be focusing on updates for the Virtual Bimbo software.

Instead of work, his mind kept circling the memories of their weekend together. An image of the smooth curves of her bare ass up against his hips as he buried his cock inside her, pounding against her again and again, flashed in his head, and he got an erection right there under the glaring fluorescent lights.

Damn it. He shifted in his seat, tugging at his khakis

to create some extra room for his wood as he turned away from the guy across the aisle from him.

Even his guilt hadn't put a damper on his desire for her. But regardless of what his body wanted, he had to put some distance between them. They couldn't keep going at it like rabbits.

"Hey," a female voice said from behind him, and Alex turned to see Yasmine standing there.

"Hey, yourself."

"Can you spare a few minutes in the break room?"

"Sure, what's up?"

She held her finger to her lips and nodded ever so slightly toward the guy sitting behind her. "Nothing much, just a little issue to clear up."

Alex watched as she turned and headed away, her tight black skirt revealing long, golden legs accented by a pair of high heels. Guys couldn't help but stare as she passed, though now, when he got up to follow, they stared at him as well.

A few people had commented on his showing up at the holiday party with Yasmine, but they were the typical guy sort of comments, nothing particularly rude. Now his co-workers looked at him as if he'd just discovered the secret to eternal life and was refusing to share it.

He couldn't say he blamed them.

Alex opened the door of the break room and entered, letting it swing shut behind him. Inside, the scent of microwave buttered popcorn mingled with the less-distinctive and less-pleasant odors of various frozen and left-over lunches that had been reheated recently. Yasmine was removing a Mountain Dew from the soda machine.

"Why do I feel like this is an illicit meeting?" he asked when she turned to him.

"I just didn't want anyone listening in. We're now the number-one fodder for office gossip, and I, for one, don't think I can take another guy giving me that *look* today."

"What look?" But he knew the one she meant.

"That 'I'm picturing you naked getting it on with one of my co-workers' look."

Alex tried not to smile. "I haven't gotten any looks like that today."

"Lucky you, but seriously, could you do me a favor and start dispelling the myths?"

"What myths?"

"Come on, now, don't tell me you haven't heard."

"Heard what?"

"Rumors about this weekend are getting out of control. People are saying we did it in a hotel rest room, that we were taking our clothes off as we climbed into the limousine to leave—"

"But we didn't even take a limo."

"Exactly."

Alex gave up his battle with the laughter building inside him. It erupted, and to his surprise, Yasmine laughed along with him.

He'd expected her to be thoroughly pissed off, offended, outraged even. But instead, she laughed deep in her belly as if he'd just told the funniest joke she'd ever heard—until her eyes were watering and her cheeks were a rosy pink. He loved that he couldn't always anticipate her reactions, and he loved that in the face of possible workplace humiliation, she could laugh.

He wondered if it was her rebellious streak coming out again, enjoying the spectacle they'd created at the same time that her more cautious side yearned to avoid controversy.

"I'm sorry," he said once she'd gotten control over herself. "I know this is annoying. Where the hell are the crazy rumors coming from?"

"You take all these guys and give them fodder for a fantasy, and what do you expect?"

"Why would they be fantasizing about us together?" he asked.

"It's more like they're fantasizing about what might be possible if they're the lucky guy the next time a holiday office party rolls around."

"Ah. I see. I'll make sure I put the rumors to rest."

"I'm not asking you to lie," she said, then took a sip of her soft drink.

"It's okay, really. The last thing I want is to make it hard for you to work here."

"Thanks. I'll do what I can to dispel any rumors I hear, too. I didn't think I cared one way or the other about this stuff, but I can't stand getting *this* much attention."

"Let's make sure we've got our stories matched up. Say we tell everyone I took you home, gave you a chaste kiss on the cheek, and that was the end of it. We're just friends, and we don't have any plans to date again."

But as the words exited his mouth, some crazy part of him wanted to take them back. He didn't want it all to be over. Didn't want the hottest affair he'd ever had to have lasted only a weekend.

"That sounds okay, I guess."

"You guess?"

She gave him a speculative look. "I know we agreed this would be a one-weekend thing, but…"

This was it. This was where he was supposed to tell her that they couldn't see each other again, that continuing what they'd started would be a mistake.

But would she hear the insincerity in his voice? Would she see it in his eyes?

"Do you really think it's a good idea to keep this up? I mean, with us working together, and the rumors already running rampant…"

She sighed and flopped down in the nearest metal folding chair. Alex kept his distance, still standing near the door where he was less tempted to slide his hand up Yasmine's shirt and under her bra.

"You're right," she said. "I knew from the start it was a bad idea."

"Some bad ideas just have to be tried anyway. And I don't regret a second of it."

"So…we just act like this weekend never happened?"

"You okay with that?"

Her gaze traveled from the green plastic bottle she held to him. "Absolutely. It's really the best way to go."

Right. It was clean and easy, and it would make living with his guilty conscience a little easier.

So why did his every male fiber protest the idea? Why did he feel like spreading her out on the break table, pushing her skirt up around her waist, and giving the employees of VirtualActive a hell of a lot more to gossip about?

Because his dick had no common sense, that's why.

Instead, he closed the distance between them and leaned over Yasmine, tilting her chin up with one hand.

He'd intended to plant a soft, friendly kiss on her cheek, thank her for everything and vow never to say a word about what they'd done....

But something entirely different happened.

His mouth disobeyed. Refused to make contact with her cheek. Went straight for the cushion of her full lips. And then his tongue launched its own rebellion, probing into her mouth, hungry for the taste of her mingled with Mountain Dew.

Then she was standing up, and his hands were buried in her hair, cupping the back of her head as their mouths completely ignored the vow they'd just made to be nothing more than friendly co-workers.

"Whoa! Sorry to interrupt. I'll just get my coffee later."

They broke apart and saw the source of their interruption. Drew was backing out the door with coffee cup in hand, his expression a mixture of embarrassment and interest.

"Um..." Yasmine said, but nothing else came out.

When the break room door had swung shut again, they looked at each other.

"Crap."

"Yeah," Alex said, feeling like a jerk. "Sorry."

"I wasn't exactly stopping you."

"You shouldn't have needed to."

"So much for putting an end to the rumors." The wry smile she wore suggested she accepted their plight as inescapable now.

"I'll tell Drew that was our farewell kiss, and that we're finished. No more making out in the break room."

"Or you could tell him I had a potato chip stuck in

my throat and you were trying to remove it with your tongue." Her laugh cut through the tension in the room.

"Have you ever had an office affair before?" Alex asked.

"No. This is my first and last."

The determination in her voice should have been some relief to him, but instead it left him feeling disappointed.

He nodded as if he knew just how she felt.

"Guess I'd better get back out to my desk before they send another spy in here," she said, flashing a tired smile as she headed for the door.

He couldn't keep going like this. He'd lied to Yasmine, and he didn't have it in him to tell her the truth. Not so soon on the heels of their lovemaking. He just needed to get away from her, get some physical and emotional distance, and then he'd be able to think clearly. Decide what to do next.

Figure out where to go and what to do after giving up what he feared he wanted most in life.

BY THE END OF THE WORKDAY Tuesday, Alex knew he had to leave VirtualActive, and the sooner the better. He couldn't keep living in the middle of this lie.

The decision had been brewing in his subconscious since last night, and being so close to Yasmine today, while knowing he should stay away from her, solidified it. Plus, there were more practical concerns, such as the fact that he'd uncovered everything he could about her hacking activities or lack thereof, and his case was as closed as it would ever be. Oh, and he couldn't forget that if he didn't turn his attention back to his information security business, it was going to go under before it had really gotten started.

He peered in the door of his supervisor's office and saw that he was free, so he gave a quick knock.

"Hey, Kyle, what's up?" Bryan Dermott asked when he looked up from his computer.

"You have a minute to talk?"

"Sure, come on in."

Alex sat on the edge of the nearest chair. "I just wanted to let you know I don't think this job is the right fit for me, and I'm putting in my notice to leave."

"Wow. Um, this is rather sudden. I hope it doesn't have anything to do with those rumors that have been flying around here today."

"No, the rumors are completely false," Alex said. "It's a personal decision, based purely on what I'm looking for in a job."

"Fair enough. If you're not happy with the work, you're not happy."

"Thanks for understanding," he said, glad to at least be getting this obstacle out of his way. Without the job, there'd be at least that distance between him and Yasmine.

"Well, since you just started a few weeks ago, and you haven't taken on that big a workload yet, we're not going to be hurting if you leave today."

"Are you sure about that?"

Bryan nodded. "You don't have to bother with two weeks' notice. Go ahead and clear out your desk, and we'll call this your last day."

This was the part where Alex was supposed to feel secretly relieved and thrilled, but a knot formed in his gut instead. It was time to move on, time to put the case behind him, time to focus on his own life and forget about all things related to Yasmine Talbot.

He left Bryan's office and walked through the aisles of cubicles, this time wishing he could avoid Yasmine's—an odd feeling after having spent the past weeks coming up with excuse after excuse to walk by her desk.

She looked up from her work and saw him as he neared.

"Hey," he said, assuming the posture of a guy who'd just been let go.

Luckily, most of the people who sat near her had just left for a training session and wouldn't be around to hear him confess his job "loss."

Her expression, distracted and vague, made it clear he'd interrupted her in the middle of some serious code slinging. "What's the matter?" she asked.

"Today's my last day here."

Her jaw dropped. "What happened?"

"I'm not as qualified for the job as I thought I was."

"But you just started. It takes time to learn everything."

"Honestly, I'm not that into it. I need a job I feel passionate about."

Two little creases formed between her eyebrows, and he wished he could reach out and smooth them.

"I guess I can understand that. This just seems so sudden— Wait a minute. This doesn't have anything to do with me, does it?"

"Of course not. It's a career decision."

Which sounded about as likely as claiming sleeping with her in the first place had been a career decision.

She sat speechless for a few moments, before he filled in the silence for her.

"I swear this has nothing to do with you. Ever since I finished training, I've been feeling like I was in the wrong job, and a talk I just had with Bryan Dermott confirmed it."

"What are you going to do?" she asked.

He shruggedd. "I'm still considering my options."

She blinked, then looked at him as if she knew there was something he wasn't telling her. "I'll miss seeing you around here," she finally said. "You really added some interest to our office landscape."

"I'll miss seeing you, too," he said, wondering if this would be the last time.

Would he have the willpower to stay away? Would she?

"So, is this it?" Yasmine asked, looking a little unsure of herself for once.

"'It' as in the last time we see each other?"

"Yeah." Her voice was soft, almost a whisper.

"Do you want it to be?"

Against all his better sense, he wanted her to say no.

"No," she said, answering his prayers.

"Neither do I."

"Then I'll call you. Or you call me, okay?"

Alex nodded and smiled. "Okay."

They stared at each other for a moment too long, something big and uncomfortable hanging in the air between them. The unstated fact that their relationship didn't have a destination. It was a bus on the road to nowhere, and neither of them wanted to get off.

13

ALEX HAD BEEN PUTTING OFF clients for weeks. Now, with no fake day job to distract him, he could finally get down to business and take care of the people who could keep him afloat financially. The problem was, work was the last thing on his mind.

He'd been sitting at his desk all morning, trying like hell to concentrate and only occasionally succeeding. He seemed to be a much greater success at catching up on his e-mail, filing papers that could have waited to be filed, and eliminating every dust particle from the surface of his desk.

It didn't help that he was working at home, and the TV was only a room away, beckoning with the promise of *Seinfeld* reruns and twenty-four-hour news. Not only that, but he'd made numerous trips to the kitchen, coming back to his desk with chips, a ham sandwich, a popsicle, too many cups of coffee and now an ill-thought-out bowl of cereal that had resulted in milk droplets on his keyboard.

At this rate, he wouldn't be able to fit through his office door in another month, and his big fat lie of an investigation would be the least of his worries.

He finally decided that the only way he was going to

get his mind off Yasmine was to give the whole issue some formal closure, so he opened his file on her and started typing notes on his conclusions about her case. There really wasn't much to type. He'd explored every avenue investigating her, and there was no evidence that she'd engaged in any form of cyber crime—messing with the terrorists wasn't really criminal—since her release from juvenile prison.

The only question left in his mind was, why did any of his former colleagues at the FBI think she was guilty of hacking? Likely because they were under pressure to produce some suspects in a world where the smart criminals were incredibly hard to catch. It was so easy to go incognito on the Internet, ten criminals got away for every one the FBI's cyber crime unit caught.

Alex had learned to accept that frustration as part of the job, but not everyone could.

And then there was Ty Connelly. Alex's subconscious kept circling back to him, wondering how he fit into the case. Ty had headed up the witch hunt against Yasmine. There was something about the whole situation that Alex was missing, some piece of the puzzle he couldn't find.

He had to talk to Ty. He couldn't put his finger on any one reason, but if nothing else, he'd turn over his notes on Yasmine's case to the agent and let him see for himself how wrong he'd been about her. He picked up the phone and dialed the number to the FBI office that he still knew by heart, and a few minutes later he had an afternoon meeting set up at a restaurant that was midway between their two locations.

He drove to the meeting filled with a dull ache,

both relieved and unnerved that he'd gotten nowhere with the case. When he reached the North Beach restaurant, he found Ty already waiting for him inside. They shook hands, exchanged greetings, then sat across from each other.

"I ordered you a cup of coffee. Hope that's okay," Ty said, nodding at the full cup on the table.

"Thanks, man."

"So what's been going on with you?"

Alex probably should have finessed the situation, engaged in a little small talk before going straight to business, but instead, he pushed the file on Yasmine across the table to Ty. "This is what's been going on with me."

Alex sipped the black coffee and then set the cup down as Ty scanned the notes.

Around them, the noise from the late lunch crowd in the restaurant created a comfortable din that ensured no one else was likely to hear their conversation, and the scents of coffee and unidentifiable foods filled the air. Instead of staring at Ty, who looked a little heavier than the last time he'd seen him, and a little more unkempt, Alex took note of the other customers in the restaurant. They were almost uniformly well-dressed, upwardly mobile pretty people.

"I thought you'd given this up, man," Ty finally said when he finished reading.

Alex shrugged. "I gave up the job, but that doesn't mean all my business was finished. I had this one loose end to tie up, and now I'm done."

"That's not the way it works, and you know it."

"There's an exception to every rule. I know this case

better than anyone, and simply handing over my files incomplete would have been irresponsible."

Ty flipped back to the photo of Yasmine on the first page and eyed it appreciatively, then shot Alex a look. "Is that really why you kept pursuing this case?"

"My reasons don't matter. What matters is, I figured out Yasmine Talbot has had no recent contact with The Underground. I think it's possible someone's trying to frame her—could be someone within the FBI."

He watched Ty's reaction, looking for something— anything.

"Damn. That's a serious accusation. Where's your proof?" Ty said, appropriately skeptical.

"That's the thing. There isn't any solid proof, and I don't know what anyone's motive would be. It's just a hunch, and I thought if I was going to take anything as shaky as a hunch to someone, it should be you."

"Thanks for bringing this to me. I'll look into it." He tucked the papers into his briefcase. "How's civilian life treating you?"

"It's not bad. I don't miss being an agent like I thought I would."

And, he realized for the first time that it was true. He hadn't missed a minute of the bureaucracy, the endless paperwork, the constant battle for staffing and funding.

"You got the right idea, man. The private sector is where it's at. Let me know if you're ever looking for a business partner."

"You? Leave the Bureau?"

Ty sipped his coffee, then sighed. "What can I say? I'm getting tired of all the crap. You can't serve twenty years without feeling a little burned out."

"I hear you."

"So you and this Yasmine chick—you finally hook up? Is that how you got your information?"

There was the question Alex had hoped like hell to avoid.

"I'm not going to lie. We were involved for a short while."

"Now there's an investigative method you can't use when you carry an FBI badge. Yet another advantage of going civilian."

Alex wanted to protest, but he'd asked for it. He'd behaved reprehensibly, and there was no point denying it.

"I can't say I'll let it happen again. It was a stupid thing to do."

"Hey, man, I bet she's one of the hottest little mistakes you'll ever make."

Alex looked out at the passing traffic, wishing he were anywhere but here bullshitting about the woman who confused him more than anything or anyone else. He didn't like hearing Ty sum up their relationship the way he had.

"You ever hear from Kinsey?" Ronald Kinsey had been dismissed from the same field office as Alex two days after Alex's resignation. Caught in the same fallout as Alex, he'd been accused of tampering with case evidence, among other lesser infractions.

"Not a word from him."

Alex had wondered if Kinsey had been the one trying to pin guilt on Yasmine, but he'd probably never know now.

"Listen, it's been good talking. I'll look into this issue with Talbot. Thanks for bringing it to me."

"You'll let me know if you come up with anything?"

"As soon as I'm able to talk, I will. It's the least I can do."

Alex left the restaurant not exactly feeling the sense of closure he'd hoped to find, but at least he had some hope now that he had finally done the right thing. He sat in his car and waited for Ty to leave, then followed him from a few car lengths, curious to see where Ty would go next. He was relieved to see that his former colleague went straight to the office. And he realized as he sat in his car staring at the FBI building in which he'd once worked that this was truly the end.

Case closed. He'd be a lunatic to continue searching for clues that weren't there, following hunches based on no solid facts.

He said a silent goodbye to his old life, pulled out into traffic and drove away.

ONLY TWO DAYS after Alex had left VirtualActive, Yasmine was having serious withdrawal symptoms. She had trouble sleeping, she'd been eating too much, and she couldn't stop replaying their weekend together in her head.

Okay, sure, they shouldn't see each other anymore, so technically, his leaving had been a good thing.

But tell that to her body. And her heart.

Her heart had decided, without consulting her brain, that Kyle was the man for her and that she was falling head over heels in love. For once she was pretty damn sure she'd found a guy who was attracted to her—all of her, and not just her appearance.

Not in the mood for exercise or explanations about

why her office hottie had disappeared, Yasmine had tried every possible excuse to get out of going to Pilates class with Cass, but in the end she'd lost the argument.

Now, though, having spent the past few days with a growing sense of unease, she was just glad for Cass's company. Another heavy-breathing phone call in the middle of the night two nights ago had set her nerves on edge. At first she'd thought Kyle was calling to have phone sex, but after a minute had passed and all she'd heard was breathing, she realized it definitely wasn't Kyle. It was the same creep who'd been calling her all along.

And last night she'd watched a car pull up outside her apartment—the same white car she'd seen there before—then sit for hours without anyone getting out, as far as she could tell. She'd gotten another phone call, this one silent, and she couldn't help wondering if it had come from the mystery car. She was probably just being paranoid.

She and Cass sat on their mats on the glossy wood floors of Studio Fitness and waited for the lithe, ridiculously flexible instructor named Noni to appear and lead them through a series of exercises that promised to leave Yasmine unable to take deep breaths without feeling it in her abs for several days.

"What is it with you and your opposition to exercise?"

"It's not exercise I dislike so much as it is this form of exercise. I mean, all this damn rolling and crunching—it's just not healthy," Yasmine whispered.

"Look around you. Do these people not look healthy?"

"Please name one occasion where I'll ever need to

fold myself in half and touch my toes to the floor over my head."

"That's not the point, but I can think of interesting uses for that pose."

Cass had been looking awfully smug this evening, and Yasmine had a feeling it was related to Drew, who'd seemed dreamy and distracted all week—and hadn't wanted to say a word about his date with Cass.

Noni was in her place at the head of the class now, and they started their warm-up breathing, which always bored the hell out of Yasmine. She pretended to go along with the exercises while she whispered to Cass, "When are you going to give me the scoop on Drew?"

A mysterious half smile played on her lips. "That's going to take a while. You'll have to wait for dinner to hear the complete story."

"Does that mean you like him?"

"Patience, my dear."

Twenty minutes into the exercise routine, Yasmine was ready to sneak out and grab a doughnut, but Cass was all about the floor work. She may not be a stripper anymore, but she still acted as though she might have to bare her ass to a roomful of men at any given moment. Yasmine didn't see the point of spending her whole life worrying about a few extra pounds here or there.

"Imagine your spine elongating as you reach up toward the sky," Noni was saying, as Yasmine tried to decide if she was more in the mood for Thai food or Mexican.

Cass would never go for Mexican after a workout, and sure enough, another half hour later when they were dressing in the locker room, she scoffed at the very idea.

"We just worked out! We need to eat something light and healthy."

"Thai is as light and healthy as I'm going to get. Want to try that place on the next block?"

"Okay, so long as you fill me in starting right now on what's happening with you and the office hottie. It must be interesting because you look like you haven't slept in days."

At the mention of sleep, Yasmine suppressed a yawn. "I'm just not sleeping well. I've started feeling like someone's watching me again."

"Oh, sweetie. I swear that's all just the residual effect of having been the object of an FBI investigation once in your life."

"But maybe they're investigating me again." Maybe they'd picked up on her little foray into crashing the terrorist Web site and had decided to make some crazy example of her again.

Or maybe Cass was right.

"Haven't you ever been in a crowded room and felt like someone was watching you, and when you looked around, you found out someone really was watching you?" Yasmine asked.

"Sure, but of course people would be watching me. I dress to impress. I think you just need to get your mind focused on something positive. Like giving me the scoop on your hot and heavy weekend, ASAP."

"Well…" Where to start? "We spent one long, blissful weekend together."

"And?"

"And lots of sex happened. Lots of talking happened. Some eating happened. More sex happened. It was fun."

"You are *so* not getting away with the *Reader's Digest* version."

They stood in front of the mirror touching up their hair and makeup, and Cass gave her a look through the mirror that let her know she meant business.

"Okay, fine," Yasmine said as she wrestled her hair into a new ponytail. "I'll give you every boring detail if you want."

"Just the important stuff."

What was the important stuff? The question had barely formed in her head when she had an answer. A big, all-caps answer that she totally hadn't wanted to admit to herself. She might have been able to lie to herself, but she couldn't lie to her best friend.

"I know this is going to sound crazy," Yasmine said, "but I'm totally falling for him."

"Falling, as in, falling in *love?*"

Hearing the word spoken out loud gave her butterflies, but it certainly didn't ring false. "I don't know if I'd go that far, but I'm definitely falling into some heavy emotions with him."

"You should write greeting cards. 'I'm falling in heavy emotions with you.'"

"Don't be a smart-ass."

Cass had stopped applying her mascara and gave Yasmine an appraising glance. "Okay, I'll admit that for you—the one who's sworn off taking risks—to be confessing to heavy emotions already? It's a big deal."

"It's scary."

"I think it's awesome."

For Cass, who generally wasn't prone to such enthusiastic exclamations, to make such a statement meant something was up. Yasmine would have wagered a bet that it had to do with her own feelings for Drew.

They left the fitness studio and headed toward the Thai restaurant, but Yasmine couldn't wait anymore for the details. "So I told you mine. Now you tell me yours."

Cass sighed. "You're so impatient. I guess I can spill now that we're away from prying ears. Drew and I have seen each other every day since Monday."

"Wow, so you're a thing, then?"

"I don't really want us to be, but I don't know. I mean, I'm starting to feel like I'm back in junior high school."

"How so?"

"I'm afraid I have that whole giddy thing going on again. I could spend all day and all night with him and still not feel like telling him to go entertain himself."

"What have you two been doing? Gazing into each other's eyes?"

"Probably a similar schedule to yours and Kyle's. Sex, talk, sex, eat, more sex, et cetera. The only reason I'm not seeing him tonight is he had to work late."

"Oh, right," Yasmine said, remembering the after-hours meeting she didn't have to attend.

"The thing is, though, I dread getting involved again, and you know why."

"I know you're happy without a guy, and that's great, but why can't you be happy with a guy, too? What's so bad about that?"

"Been there, done that, sweetie. Happy quickly leads to miserable."

"Maybe all those other guys were just practice for the real thing."

"Haven't we already had this talk? I don't *want* the real thing. I just want an occasional itch scratched, so why should I buy a whole tree when I can just go outside and rub up against any old branch anytime I want?"

Yasmine blinked at Cass's wacked logic. "If you really just want sex, and that's what makes you happy… then, I guess you're right."

"Thank you for understanding. Now the problem remains that I like Drew and don't really want to get rid of him."

"Told you you'd like him!"

"No need to be smug. He's a sweet guy. I'd hate to break his heart."

"You have to tell him what you're looking for. Maybe he'd be okay with just being your, um, branch," Yasmine said, looking left and right as they started to cross the street.

She was trying to sound supportive of Cass's choices and all, but it struck her then how different she and her friend really were. Cass might have been totally happy living alone and without a partner, but Yasmine wanted the opposite. She'd been trying to live a life without close ties, without emotional entanglements, for fear of getting hurt, and it wasn't working. Her weekend with Kyle had given her a taste of what she was missing.

"I guess you're right. I'm just afraid of hurting his feelings. I never would have thought I'd go for a computer geek…. But the sex—oh mama, the sex is to die for."

"That's all the info I need, thanks."

"I mean, the man eats pussy like it's filet mignon—"

"Whoa there! Lalalalalalala—I don't want to hear

any more. I've got to work with Drew, and I'd like to remain friends with both of you."

"Oh, you're such a prude."

"I just think certain facts about a relationship need to remain private. But regardless, maybe he'll be happy to be at your service. You never know."

They reached the restaurant, went inside and found a table as the Seat Yourself sign instructed.

Once they were seated, Cass leveled a look at Yasmine that made her want to slide under the table.

"What?" she hazarded to ask.

"We've been friends so long, I'm starting to sound like you with all these worries."

"You don't sound like me. You sound like a very confused woman."

"Exactly. Your problem is, you're afraid of everything, and I think you're starting to rub off on me."

"That's crazy. What am I afraid of?"

"You might think you're Miss Thing with your bad attitude and your rebel-without-a-cause posture, but you're not fooling me."

Yasmine's lips parted, but no words came out. She wanted to argue with Cass, tell her how wrong she was, but deep down a little nagging voice said her friend might be right.

"What does this have to do with anything?"

"I'm the one with the irregular emotional wiring, not you. I'm the one who's perfectly happy alone. You, on the other hand, are afraid that if you fall in love, you'll be the one who gets hurt later. You're afraid to put yourself out there."

"So what's wrong with not wanting to get hurt?"

"You're not living! It's like ever since you got out of that kiddy prison, you've decided to keep yourself locked up in a prison of your own making."

Yasmine's instincts went on alert. Cass had seen a part of Yasmine she'd been keeping so guarded, she hadn't even remembered it existed. "That's crazy."

"My point exactly," her friend said, nodding in triumph.

"No, I mean, it's not true. I can't believe you'd think that about me." And Yasmine couldn't believe she was lying to her own best friend, but she felt as though her dirtiest little secret had just been announced to the world, and she'd been caught completely unprepared.

Cass's eyebrows quirked, a telltale sign that she didn't buy a word of Yasmine's story. "Okay, let's do a little 'decade in review' then."

"Let's don't."

She ignored Yasmine and continued. "First, Yasmine is released from juvenile detention. Then she forgoes her plans to attend Stanford and instead goes to Cal State. While there, she lives a low-key existence, studies hard and graduates a year early. Nothing else of note happens in her life—no torrid love affairs, no unkempt treks through Europe, very little drunken excess to speak of. All of her relationships are with safe, emotionally unavailable bad boys, meaning no commitment required. Upon graduation, she takes the first job she can find at a sex software company, of all places, and she continues working there, with no notable events occurring in her life, until now."

Yasmine frowned. "You make me sound so boring."

"That's just it. You're one of the most interesting people I know, and yet you're living the most boring life. Don't you ever stop to ask yourself why?"

"I just want to stay out of trouble."

Oddly, unexpectedly, Yasmine was struck with a wave of sadness. It was as if she felt that she needed to mourn the life she'd been failing to live. All this time she thought she'd been a bad girl trying to be good, when really she'd tamed herself to the point of being no kind of girl at all. Just an empty shell, devoid of all the stuff she hoped people would see in her. No wonder guys focused on her outward appearance—there wasn't anything left inside to appreciate.

She felt her lower lip quivering, which was possibly the most idiotic thing she'd done all week.

"Oh, sweetie, what is it? I didn't mean to upset you."

Yasmine took a sip of the water a hurried waitress had placed on the table before rushing off. The drinking gave her a chance to regain her composure.

"How did this go from your Drew dilemma to a dissection of my life?"

Cass made a little half smile. "You know how I hate being under the microscope. I'm sorry I upset you."

"You were hoping I'd jump for joy at the news that my life is dull and meaningless?"

"I just thought you needed to hear the truth. I don't want you to throw away your life trying so hard to stay out of trouble. You're a good person who made a mistake."

"No, I'm a bad person who's learned how to control my impulses."

"You just keep telling yourself that."

"And what?"

"You can grow old bored and alone. Is that what you want?"

Yasmine downed the rest of her water as she stared

across the room at the restaurant full of couples and friends smiling, talking, looking happy. When was the last time she'd sat in a restaurant looking happy with a guy she was in love with?

The awful truth slapped her in the face. She'd never been in love. She'd dated, she'd had lovers, and she'd sat in restaurants with them, probably on the outside looking as though they were a happy couple. But in the end, those affairs had always fizzled out, fueled by nothing more than the quick burst of passion that faded as quickly as fireworks.

"Of course not. I don't want to be alone."

"So do you think you'll be ready to tell Kyle the big *L* word anytime soon?"

Yasmine couldn't help it, she smiled. "Who knows. Anything's possible, right?"

"Like maybe… On New Year's Eve, as you ring in the new year?"

"Ohh, that's way too soon. But it would be romantic. Assuming he feels the same way."

And what if he did? What if he felt some kind of heavy emotions, too? She had to know for sure, so she decided right then and there that yes, she'd see Kyle again soon, and she'd take a risk. She'd tell him how she really felt.

She couldn't think of a better way to start off the new year.

14

ALEX RUBBED HIS EYES and leaned back in his desk chair, tired of working and tired of being alone. Avoiding Yasmine sucked. Not having her around sucked, not making love to her sucked, and leaving all his lies hanging between them sucked most of all.

He couldn't focus on work until he told her the truth—that much was becoming painfully apparent. He needed to call her, go see her, find the guts to tell her everything and ask her forgiveness. Maybe once she finished being pissed off at him, they'd have a chance. Or maybe not, but he had to tell her regardless of the consequences.

He had just picked up the phone and started dialing her number when the doorbell rang. Alex put down the phone and went to the door, his heart pounding in his chest when he saw that it was Yasmine.

As if she'd been reading his mind.

"Hey," he said when he opened the door.

"Hey, yourself." She smiled and reached for him, stood on tiptoes to give him a long, hot kiss.

"To what do I owe this pleasure?"

"I hate not seeing you at the office, and I was in your neighborhood for an exercise class and thought I'd stop in."

"I've missed you," he said as he closed the door behind her.

She shrugged off her green leather jacket, and he took it and hung it on the coat rack. "Hope I'm not interrupting anything."

"No, I was just sitting here thinking about you, actually."

She flashed a smile. "You were?"

"Yeah," he said. "We need to talk."

She slipped her fingers into his belt loop and pulled him toward her. "Did I mention that I'm really, really horny?"

This was where he should put some distance between them, stay his course....

"I've been thinking of you all day." She slid her hands around his waist and gripped his ass, massaging as she talked. "Thinking about what I'd like to be doing with you."

"Oh, yeah?" His cock went erect against her, and when he recalled her peep show performance, he wanted, more than anything, to have her again.

He'd never met a woman so hot, so right for him, so absolutely tempting....

He summoned his deepest reserve of willpower, but a voice inside his head said this was his last chance with her. That the one thing that could best remind her how right they were together was to make love to her.

He knew it was wrong, but he couldn't stop himself from this wanting that wouldn't be controlled. Not when the woman he wanted more than air was right here in his arms, warm and willing.

He gave in and kissed her, a kiss that was all wanting and hunger. He dragged her over to the couch, and they fumbled with buttons and zippers, undressing in a frenzy until it was just skin on skin. Yasmine pushed him back onto the couch, climbed on his lap.

The pent-up desire of the past few days apart had them all over each other like starving people, and Yasmine's naked body was his feast. He devoured her breasts, savoring her hard nipples in his mouth, but he needed more—needed to drink her juices, taste her all over.

He stretched out on the couch and urged Yasmine on top of him with her legs straddling his neck, but she turned around, found his cock as she offered him her pussy. And as he thrust his tongue into her, she took him into her mouth, giving him twice the pleasure he'd imagined, twice the intimacy.

He drank her in until she was quivering against him, but if he let her continue pleasuring him, he'd explode. And so he had to stop. Had to work his way inside her. He lifted her off and sat up, then pulled her onto his lap. In his wallet was a condom, and Yasmine found it before he did, slid it on him, and he eased into her slowly, savoring her sweet tightness.

Cupping her ass, he set the rhythm of her rocking hips, and he watched the pleasure play across her face as he quickened their pace.

Her flesh against him, his flesh inside of her, their shared pleasure—it was perfect. It was what he'd always imagined sex could be with the right woman. This was as good as it got, and more than he should have taken.

Banishing the truth edging in on his fantasy, he pulled her closer and held her face in his hands as he kissed her through the last delicious thrusts. Her body tensed, tightened around him, and she cried out in release.

His own orgasm came on the heels of hers, almost violent as it shuddered through his body. He clung to her, spilling into her, wishing this closeness wouldn't end.

When they'd both caught their breath, he kissed her deep and slow, then eased her onto the couch beside him, tucking her against his body, where she fit all too perfectly.

"I'm glad you stopped by," he said.

She smiled. "I noticed. I like the way you say hello."

"I didn't mean for us to get carried away like that, but we seem to have a certain effect on each other."

"What's wrong with getting carried away?" she asked, nudging him with her hip.

"Normally, I'm all for it. But I need to talk to you, and I've been putting it off too long."

"I've been meaning to talk to you, too," she said. "I was going to wait until New Year's Eve, but after what just happened, I think now is as good a time as any."

She turned her body toward him and sat up on her elbow, looking him in the eyes.

"What's up?" he asked, fear churning in his gut. What if she was already on to him, and he didn't get a chance to come clean first...?

"This might sound crazy, but you and me—us, this thing that's happening between us." She sighed, smiling as she traced a finger along his lower lip. "I think I'm falling for you."

The fear in his stomach turned to stone, and suddenly he couldn't remember how to breathe. The words, spoken aloud, made perfect sense, and he knew in that instant he was falling in love with her, too. But she didn't even know his real name, or the impact he'd had on her life.

He'd never meant for it to happen this way.

"I'm falling for you, too, Yasmine. But you have to hear me out."

Her smile faded. "You sound so serious."

He sat up and pulled her up with him, holding her hands in his. "This is serious," he said, then took a deep breath. It was now or never. "I haven't been honest with you, and I need to explain why."

"What haven't you been honest about?"

"I'm not who you think I am," Alex said.

She expelled a nervous laugh. "What? You're really a secret agent, infiltrating my life to see if I'm hacking into government computers?"

When he didn't laugh, her expression went from tentative to concerned.

"Not exactly," he said.

"Kyle? What the hell does 'not exactly' mean?"

Damn it, he hated himself right now.

"My name's not really Kyle," he said as he held her hands tighter, hoping she wouldn't run away, forcing himself to breathe evenly. "It's Alex. Alex DiCarlo."

She blinked and shook her head, as if her brain was circling his words, trying to make sense of them. Did his name sound familiar to her?

Did it linger in her mind as a sentence in the worst chapter of her life? Did she ever see his face in her memory, on the witness stand?

Her mind registered the words, and she jerked her hands away, then crossed her arms over her chest.

"Why the hell did you lie to me about your name? Who's Kyle Kramer?"

"Just a name I made up. I lied because I didn't want you to recognize me," he forced himself to say.

"I don't get it."

"Do you remember the FBI agent who testified against you during your trial?"

Two vertical creases formed on her brow. "Sort of. I mean, I have a vague memory…."

Her eyes widened as she stared at him. And her mouth opened as if she were about to say something, but no words emerged.

"Do you recognize me now?"

"You're the one?"

"That was me. I testified against you. I worked on the case and gathered the evidence that helped convict you." He said the words in a gush of air before he could stop, lose his nerve, forget all about honor and honesty so he could hold on to this woman.

She sprang up from the couch, her gaze searching him for some hint of his old appearance. "You? But you don't look the same."

"I grew my hair longer, it got bleached out in the sun, and I got colored contact lenses."

He wanted to take her in his arms and hold her, get rid of that growing look of betrayal darkening her features, but it wouldn't do any good.

"Why? Why are you here in disguise? Sleeping with me, pretending you're someone else!"

"I'm sorry. I'm so sorry I lied to you. You were one of the suspects in a case I was investigating before I left the FBI. I had to know if you were really involved, and

I had to know if I'd really let myself miss the facts because of my attraction to you. I'll admit, there was some desire for revenge involved at first. If you were guilty, I wanted to be the one to prove it, out of some stupid sense of pride."

"And you slept with me to find out the truth?"

"No. Not exactly."

"Are you still an agent?"

"No, I was forced to resign six months ago."

"For your creative investigating methods?"

"I didn't intend to sleep with you. At least not at first, not until I realized how attracted we were to each other."

"Why are you all of a sudden coming clean?"

"Because this has become a hell of a lot more than a weekend fling. I know you're not involved in any illegal activities, and I just want us to have a real chance together."

"Why the hell are you still investigating me if you're not an agent anymore?"

"I lost my career over this case. I needed to know the truth—"

"You bastard," she said, her voice barely controlled as she grabbed her clothes from the floor and started putting them on.

"Let's not end it like this. Please don't leave. Stay and talk to me."

"Still hoping I might know something that could get you your job back? Or are you angling to get another farewell screw?"

"No, I just want a chance to prove to you I'm not a bad person."

"And then what? We can reminisce about old times?

You can remind me what it was like during the trial? How you were so busy lusting after your sixteen-year-old suspect you could hardly pay attention to the facts of the case?"

"That's not true. I was just doing my job, and I never let anything interfere with that."

Finished dressing, she tugged her boots on and grabbed her coat from the rack. "I can't believe you just slept with me, *before* you told me your big fat secret. What the hell kind of move was that?"

"A damn stupid one. I'm sorry. I wasn't thinking with the right head."

She jerked open the door and turned back to him with fire in her eyes. "Go to hell," she said. "And when you get there, don't even think of calling me with a weather report."

He watched as she closed the door, the weight of failure sitting on his chest, making it hard to breathe. He couldn't have messed this up any more than he already had. Couldn't have made things much worse or had any crappier timing.

Damn it, he'd screwed up.

And yet, even in his failure, he felt a tiny sense of relief that he'd been right all along. She wasn't involved, wasn't the criminal he'd suspected. He hadn't let his attraction to her cloud his judgment, as had been claimed. He'd been right.

It was cold comfort.

YASMINE DROVE HOME with tears streaming down her cheeks, a white-knuckled grip on the steering wheel and her foot too heavy on the gas pedal.

She'd been so stupid.

Everything made more sense now. The eerie feeling that she'd known Kyle—Alex, whatever the hell his name was—from somewhere before, his odd behavior at his apartment that first night, as if he was trying to hide something from her, and his midnight use of her computer.

She'd been an utter and complete fool.

She'd let down her guard, had sex with him as though he was the last man on earth, and even let herself start falling in love with him.

With a guy whose name she hadn't even known. A guy who'd once testified against her. A guy she'd been foolish enough to think could see past her surface, when really he'd been obsessed with the way she looked for a decade.

She should have trusted her instincts. He was just like every other guy who'd been mesmerized by her appearance to great detriment. And maybe she'd brought that on herself, unwilling as she was to change the way she looked. Maybe she liked being pretty, but she hated that no one bothered to look deeper.

When she pulled into the parking spot in front of her apartment building, she couldn't remember how she'd gotten there. She went to her apartment and undressed without thinking. Went into the bathroom and turned on the shower, undressed and got in to wash off every trace of Alex DiCarlo from her body.

She jerked the shower curtain closed and submitted to the assault of the showerhead's spray of near-scalding water. She wanted to wash away the past week, wash away the emotions, wash away all the hope she'd managed to build up in such a short period of time.

How she'd let herself be lied to so brazenly, seduced so thoroughly, she couldn't begin to understand. And how could a relationship built on lies have felt so good and so real to her? How could she have had the feelings she did for a man she barely knew, if it was all lies?

The lengths he'd gone to—changing his name and his appearance, insinuating himself in to her workplace and then in to her bed—horrified her. Her stomach churned, and she closed her eyes as the water sprayed her face, washing away tears.

To think of how far she'd gone in their sexual relationship…. Her face burned as she recalled the peep show. She'd never put herself so far out there, never acted with such a lack of inhibition. Alex had made her feel comfortable enough to do almost anything, and now everything they'd done embarrassed the hell out of her.

She didn't want to remember any of it.

Old memories crowded out new ones as she tried to picture Alex ten years ago. She'd been so young, so scared, so far in over her head back then. Remembering the time of her trial always brought back a feeling of loss. She'd known she was losing a year of her life, a year that should have been filled with senior portraits, parties, prom, football games—all the normal stuff kids did.

She'd lost it all.

Instead, that year had been filled with a drab white room in a drab beige building. Windows with bars and kids with scars, both internal and external, that kids so young shouldn't have had. She hadn't fit in with most of those kids.

And they'd sensed her privileged upbringing. Persecuted her for it.

Maybe she'd deserved it.

She'd spent the year being stoic and reclusive, trying to keep to herself and fending off the harassment of her less-privileged peers. For months a group of girls had threatened her and jeered at her, until one day they'd caught her in a rest room and cut off all her hair, hair that had hung to her waist back then, too. She'd grown it back and still wore it that long partly as an act of defiance and partly as a security blanket.

And now in the shower was when her hair felt heaviest, weighed down with water, and she imagined cutting it all off again. Imagined letting go of it, becoming someone new, the way Alex had.

But she wouldn't. She was who she was, and she'd never disguise herself. She'd learned to live with her scarlet letter, and her hair was a part of that, too. It made her unmistakably recognizable to people who'd seen photos of her in newspapers all those years ago, and she'd gotten to a place in her life where she didn't care anymore.

She'd gotten past being the subject of an FBI investigation. It was a part of her, but it was in the past. Just like Alex. He was a ghost from her past that she needed to put to rest, and one way or another she'd get over him and move on.

15

YASMINE LIKED TO SPEND the last few days of the year deep-cleaning her apartment, so that when the new year began, she could start totally fresh. It was possibly her most anal-retentive habit, one she avoided mentioning to her friends for fear of coming off sounding like her own mother, who, although she generally didn't do the cleaning herself, insisted on a spotless household.

Today Yasmine's cleaning was fueled by rage, and her wood floors had already reached a level of shine that presented issues for the cat, who kept seeing his reflection in the floor and freaking out.

She didn't want to think about Alex, didn't want to keep being mad about him, so she took out her anger on the dirt.

When her doorbell rang around noon, and Yasmine opened the door and saw an FBI badge glinting in front of her, she felt as if she'd been struck in the chest. All this time, she'd been a law-abiding citizen, and she'd sworn to herself she'd never cross paths with the Feds again.

She'd never wanted to see another one of those badges.

The first thought that flashed in her mind was that Alex had told the authorities about her hacking into terrorist Web sites…but what would be the point of his doing that?

"Ms. Talbot, I'm Agent Connelly. I'm a field agent for the FBI's National Infrastructure Protection Center, and we have some questions for you about your recent Internet activities."

Yasmine gripped the door frame to steady herself.

It struck her only now that maybe Alex had lied about more than just his name. Maybe he'd lost his job because he was a crooked agent, and maybe he was trying to frame her for something. She'd been so dumb, she hadn't even checked out her computer after he'd used it, and now, for all she knew, he could have set her up for any number of false accusations.

"I haven't done anything wrong. I'm not a hacker anymore," she said, her mind turning over possibilities.

Just how far could Alex have gone? And if he had set her up, why did he do it?

"I understand, Ms. Talbot. But I'll need you to come with me. You answer our questions, and then you'll be free to go."

She considered saying no, saying she'd only talk with an attorney present, but really, she hadn't done anything wrong, and some niggling urge to prove it won out over her reservations.

"Fine. Let me just grab my shoes and purse," she said as she left the door.

After tugging on her boots and grabbing her bag, she followed the agent down to his car and got in the passenger side, then buckled up. It all felt eerily similar to the first time she'd ever been brought in for questioning. Only, then she'd been scared out of her mind, barely able to breathe, on the verge of tears throughout the ordeal.

They had to have seen she was just a scared kid, a spoiled brat teenager with too much time on her hands, but then again, maybe they hadn't. They'd wanted to prove a point with her, show the world that the FBI was cracking down on hackers regardless of their ages or seeming harmlessness.

At least now she wasn't so scared, and she knew what to expect.

Agent Connelly got in on the driver's side and started the car. As he steered it out into the street, she tried not to let her nerves get the best of her. He headed south, and it only took a moment for Yasmine to remember that the FBI field office was in the opposite direction. Unless they'd moved it.

"Why are we going this way?" she asked.

He cast a glance at her, then turned his attention back to the street. "I'm trying to avoid traffic."

She stared straight ahead, a lump of doubt forming in her belly as her neighborhood passed outside the car window. Maybe she was wrong. Maybe he knew some roundabout shortcut. Or maybe she didn't really understand what was going on here. Maybe she shouldn't have gotten into this car at all. A film of perspiration formed on her upper lip, in spite of the cool temperature.

The only thing he would avoid by going this way was a route to his claimed destination.

And then it occurred to her. Agents always seemed to come in pairs. From what she'd seen, they never worked alone when handling suspects.

"Where's your partner?" she said. "Aren't you supposed to have one whenever you deal with the public?" Even as the words formed in her mouth, the feeling grew in her that something was not right.

Agent Connelly stared straight ahead, silent for a moment too long. "He's sick today."

She was stupid. Stupid, stupid, stupid. Hadn't she learned anything in her entire life? Like never get into a car with a stranger?

She glanced around, looking for clues. To what, she didn't know. Finally, anger overwhelmed fear and she knew she couldn't go anywhere with this man.

"You're lying. Who the hell are you?" She gripped the door handle, peering ahead for the next stop light where she could jump out of the car.

Agent Connelly's hand dipped into his jacket, and he withdrew a gun, then rested it in his lap aimed at her with one hand as he continued to steer with the other.

"You're not going anywhere, so don't even think of jumping out."

Yasmine's throat constricted and her stomach turned sour. Fear iced through her limbs until she felt cold all over.

"What do you want with me?" Her voice came out sounding tight and near hysterical.

"Like I said, I'm just taking you in for questioning."

"Then why are we still heading in the opposite direction of the FBI office?"

"I never said I was taking you there."

"Then where?"

"Someplace private where you can provide me with the information I need."

"I don't know anything."

"You know plenty about accessing places you shouldn't, don't you?"

"I don't do that anymore, I told you!"

"But you still know how."

"What difference does that make?"

"You help me gain the access I need to certain information, and I'll let you go. After I'm finished with you."

He glanced at her then, and his gaze felt unclean, as if just by looking at her he was soiling her.

"Who are you?"

"I've been watching you. I know everything about you. I know you've been screwing my former partner, when you should have been screwing me. He's always the one women notice, but I'm the one you'll remember most."

His words registered a few at a time. Penetrating her anger, then her fear and sinking in deeper still. He'd been watching her. He was Alex's former partner. So he was, or had been, an actual FBI agent. And his intentions were far from good.

She tried to imagine how he knew she'd been sleeping with Alex. Had he bugged her apartment? Had he been in contact with Alex? Could it be that they were still working together somehow?

No. He sounded genuinely pissed off at Alex. And she couldn't let herself believe right now that Alex was capable of that depth of betrayal.

She had to get away.

But for now, while the car was moving too fast for her to make a move, she had to distract him.

"Why me?" she asked. "Why did you pick me?"

"I've had my eye on you for years. I saw your picture in the paper when you were a teenage wet dream, and I knew back then that I'd have you someday."

She bit her lip to keep from saying anything. Of all the reasons she had to be sorry for her childhood mistakes, this one had just gotten bumped up to number one. She knew she'd attracted the attention of some creepy guys, but after all these years, she'd thought that was behind her.

"I wrote to you back then, told you what I wanted to do to you. But you never answered me. So now I've had a lot of years to think of all the things I want to do with you."

Memories of all the creepy e-mails she'd gotten came flooding back to her. She tried to recall if any one stood out to her as more disturbed than the others, but she'd done her best to forget details like that. And she'd always deleted the sleazy messages back then—never dwelled on them.

"Why now? Why wait all this time?"

"I would have left you alone if it weren't for Alex. He just had to chase after you, just had to stir things up…."

His tone had turned harder, and she watched his one-handed grip on the steering wheel tighten. Her gaze dropped to the gun, cradled in his left hand, and her stomach knotted again. She fought off the urge to vomit.

Focus. She had to stay calm and focused.

Yasmine saw that the next light was green, and her stomach twisted into a tighter knot. She had no idea how she could escape with a gun pointed at her, anyway, unless she caught him off guard. Unless she jumped when he wasn't expecting it.

Which would be painful as hell, especially considering they were passing cars parked on the curb. Maybe she couldn't even jump out safely. But she glanced over at the gun, at the grim set of Agent Connelly's jaw. And she knew he wouldn't let her go. No one pulled a gun on a person he intended to have a friendly agreement with. No one made sexual threats toward a woman he didn't intend to harm.

She had to find a place to jump out, maybe at an intersection during a green light.

But her unlocking the door would alert him to her intentions. So she'd have to distract him somehow. She mentally inventoried the contents of her purse for anything that might catch him off guard, but unless she could disarm him with a tube of lipstick, she was out of luck there.

Her gaze settled on a cup of coffee in the cup holder between their seats. Steam rose up through the small hole in the plastic lid. Still hot. But could she reach for it without him getting an itchy trigger finger?

The radio volume was turned low, and a barely audible talk show played over the car's speakers. Could she turn up the volume without him getting suspicious? Maybe ask to change the station?

Too risky.

They passed a homeless man wearing an orange coat and pushing a child's stroller piled high with garbage, and Yasmine watched as he wandered into the street. Their car slowed to a stop at a red light, while the homeless man continued making his way between the parked cars and the traffic on the street.

Agent Connelly spotted him, too, just as he headed for the rear of the car. "Damn homeless, ruining the city," he said as the light turned green and he let his foot off the brake.

This was her chance, probably as distracted as he was going to get. He was still watching the homeless guy in the rearview mirror. The man had wandered into the lane behind them and was blocking traffic.

Yasmine said a little prayer, reached for the coffee cup, and grabbed it. With her other hand she flipped off the flimsy plastic lid, then hurled the cup toward Agent Connelly's face. He yelped in pain and let loose with a string of curses as he swiped at his face with his arm that held the gun. The car slowed as his foot slipped off the gas.

Without another thought, she slammed her hand down onto the automatic lock, grabbed the door handle, and jerked open the car door, realizing only as she tried to jump out the door that she was still wearing her seat belt.

Damn it.

Her hands shook as she fumbled with the seat belt lock, sparing a glance at Agent Connelly, whose face had turned an ugly red as he swiped at it, gun still in hand.

"You bitch!" she heard him say as she freed herself from the seat belt.

Then the sound of a gunshot drowned out all other sound, and searing pain invaded her thigh. Sheer force of will propelled her from the car, dragging her leg like a dead, throbbing weight. She slammed against the asphalt and started rolling forward, her skin burning along with her leg now.

In the chaos she heard another gunshot. And she scrambled to her knees, then her feet, and ran without regard for the pain in her leg between the parked cars, around the parking meters and pedestrians who had stopped to gawk, only a few thinking clearly enough to run or hide.

"Hey, do you need help?" someone called after her.

But she couldn't stop yet. She had to get away.

Down the street to the next corner, up the cross street, through a parking lot and into a shoe store where she'd once bought a pair of cross trainers. The employee behind the counter took one look at her bloody leg and came rushing out to help.

"Call 911," she said as she sank onto the nearest bench, shaking and out of breath.

The shoe salesman turned back to the counter and dialed. "Have you been shot?" he asked as he waited for an answer.

"Yes, once in the leg." And now that she took a look at herself, she saw that her other leg was bleeding, too. Her jeans had ripped away when she hit the asphalt, baring her skin to the rough surface, and it looked as if she'd left some of it behind on the street. Her arm was scraped and bloody too, and judging by the burning sensation on her cheek and brow, she had to assume her face had met a similar fate.

The salesman put the operator on hold after having a short conversation. "We need to stop the bleeding. An ambulance is on the way."

"Do you have a place in back? The guy who shot me might still be out there."

"We have some towels and a first-aid kit in the break room." He helped her up from the bench and supported her as they walked to the back.

Outside, she could hear a police siren in the distance, and she wondered for the first time what kind of scene she'd left behind her. Thank heaven for that homeless guy, or she might not have gotten out with just a gunshot wound in her thigh.

In the safety of the store's break room, she sat down and felt herself get dizzy, then decided to rest her head on the table. Her leg hurting like hell, her face and arm burning from where she'd smacked the road, nausea churning her stomach, she stayed there while the salesman assured the 911 operator that he'd followed their instructions. She sat in a daze until sirens sounded right outside the store and men in uniforms rushed in and started tending to her.

Minutes later she was in an ambulance, on a gurney, on her way to the hospital, and she was finally able to relax and drift off into the comfort of darkness.

CASS SAT IN THE PASSENGER SEAT of Drew's car, in love as always with the sight of the Golden Gate Bridge, the rust-colored pillars towering above them as they crossed it. Once they'd crossed into Marin County, Drew took the Marin Headlands exit, and they headed west, away from the main road.

It was the night before New Year's Eve, and Drew had been acting kind of funny all evening, as though he had ants in his pants or something on his mind. She tried not to think about what it might mean.

Because, much as she enjoyed their sexual relationship, the looming complications were stressing her out, and she wanted out before things got too heavy. Drew was too sweet a guy to have his heart broken by the likes of Cass. She was just waiting for the right time to tell him that he had two options with her—strictly sex or nothing at all.

She had to admit that she got an uneasy feeling about this whole situation. She might already be too late in avoiding complications. Drew's carefully selected outfit, his haircut, their well-thought-out evening together—on top of his antsy state of mind—all added up to trouble.

Drew navigated the car along the narrow road bordering the coast. Cass had been here once before, maybe as a kid. The city was visible across the bay, and as they headed farther out, she knew that even the Farrallon Islands could be seen on the horizon ahead on a clear day.

They passed a picnic area, and Drew stopped the car where the road ended at a scenic lookout point that was uninhabited by other people at the moment. It was one of those rare places near the city where a person could go and actually hope to be alone.

"Been here before?" he asked when he killed the engine.

"Maybe once. It's been forever, though. What made you think of coming out here?"

He smiled and gave her an odd look. "Get out of the car."

"You didn't bring me out here to kill me, did you?"

"Not a chance."

Outside the car, wind whipped Cass's hair into her face, and she pulled her leather coat closed tightly, then fastened the top button. She wrapped the red wool scarf that had been draped around her collar a little tighter as she walked to the fenced-off edge of the gravel parking area.

Down below, waves churned against the rocks, and though the sky was a deepening blue as the sun sank lower and lower past the horizon, while the ocean, as always, looked dark and brooding. A couple of seagulls squawked nearby, while a third poked along on the ledge, probably waiting for them to produce some food.

Drew came up behind her and slipped his hands around her waist, pulling her to him and warming her backside. He kissed the side of her neck and nestled his face against her.

"You have any New Year's resolutions?" he asked.

"Every year I say I'm going to work out six times a week or stop eating junk food or be nicer to my mother or all three, and none of it ever happens. This year I think I'll go for simplicity."

"Meaning?"

"Meaning I want to make a resolution I can actually keep."

"How about spending more time with me?" he asked, his tone teasing, though Cass got the feeling he was doing anything but.

Before she could answer he added, "Exclusively as my girlfriend?"

Cass's throat seized up. Did people actually ask for exclusive agreements anymore? It seemed like such a quaint gesture, like offering her his class ring.

"Hmm," she said, scrambling to think of an appropriately gentle response but producing nothing.

"What does that mean?"

"Oh, nothing. I'm just a little caught off guard. I mean, we only met last week."

"I'm thirty-six. I can figure out pretty quickly by now if I like a woman or not."

"I have no doubt we like each other. I just don't

think an exclusive arrangement is really...what I'm looking for."

"You want to date other men?"

"No, not at all," she said, turning to face him, wanting to make sure he saw her smile, fake as it might have been. "But what if your Miss Perfect comes along—"

Wrong thing to say. His expression turned hard. "I thought she already had."

"I can guarantee you, I'm not your Miss Perfect."

"Cass, I know what I feel."

"You feel a fuzzy-headed, misguided sense of affection brought on by intense feelings of lust."

"No, that's not it." He took her hands in his and gave her a look that said he was all business.

Damn it. She should have seen this disaster coming a mile away. She should have taken precautions to avoid it—acted a little flakier, not put so much of herself into the sex, not let down her guard so easily.

Damn it, damn it, damn it.

"I'm really into you, Cass. Like it or not, I am, and I don't need any more time to know it. I thought we were on the same page there. And I want to give us a chance."

All the air whooshed out of her lungs, and if Drew hadn't been holding on to her, the wind might have knocked her over.

"I'm sorry, Drew." She shook her head, tears welling up in the corners of her eyes. He was a sweet guy, and she didn't want to hurt him, but... "I thought we were just having some fun."

The seagull that had been skulking around nearby edged closer, possibly contemplating whether it could eat their fingers if they didn't produce any food. Cass's gaze focused on it instead of Drew.

"So what? You're not interested in making this exclusive?"

"I'm not interested in relationships at all. I've tried the romance thing and, honestly, I'm happier without it."

She didn't want to see the disappointment in his eyes, but there it was, clear as the sky above them.

His hands fell away from her, and he took a step back. "I didn't realize—"

"No, I should have told you right up front."

"I'd better take you home, then."

Cass's mouth hung open, words failing her. There had to be something she could say to fix this. Something witty, something sexy, something kind.

"We could still have dinner together."

"I don't see the point," his said with a shrug. He was trying to sound casual, but beneath the light tone there was something else.

She knew that tone. She'd heard it before, and she'd used it herself. She'd hurt him worse than he was letting on.

"Drew, please don't be upset. All I'm saying is, I'm not wired like other women. I really love being alone."

"That's fair, but I do have all the normal wiring. I want a relationship to go along with the sex, and I really don't understand how you couldn't."

Cass's stomach twisted. She didn't expect him to understand, but she hated hurting him nonetheless.

"I'm sorry," she said. "I didn't mean for things to turn out this way."

She went to the car and got in, then sat staring out the window at the stunning scenery ahead. She'd gotten what she wanted, right? She'd eliminated the possibility of future complications with Drew. So why did getting what she wanted feel like total crap?

16

THE CALL CAME to Alex on his cell phone. A former colleague from the FBI called to tell him Agent Connelly had been arrested and that Yasmine had been hurt.

Of all the stupid mistakes Alex had made regarding Yasmine, this was by far the stupidest. He'd screwed up again when he'd tried to fix things, and he should have foreseen all that could go wrong.

As he raced across town to the hospital, his insides churning at the thought of Yasmine hurt, he realized how much he'd come to care for her. She wasn't just someone he was falling in love with.

She was the one woman he'd wanted since he'd first laid eyes on her. He'd been falling in love with her for years, and knowing her now only sealed the deal. He was head over heels, and there was no way around the fact.

The words kept echoing in his head. *Yasmine was shot. She's in the E.R. at San Francisco General.*

She'd been shot. That horrible fact played itself over and over in his mind. She was recovering, but she'd been shot, and Alex had failed to protect her, had led Connelly right to her, had endangered Yasmine's life with his own desire for her.

How badly was she hurt? How long would it take her

to recover? He imagined the worst—imagined internal damage worse than their hopeless love affair could ever have caused, worse than anyone would want to reveal over the phone.

And the thought of her lying in the hospital injured caused his chest to grow tight, his throat to constrict, his breath to be fast and shallow.

By the time he found Yasmine in the E.R., resting with her leg, arm and face bandaged, he'd already managed to scare himself half to death with her imagined injuries.

When she spotted him in the doorway, she didn't smile, but she didn't alert security, either. "Hi," she said without any emotion.

He was at the side of her bed instantly. "What happened?"

"Oh, nothing much. Just got myself kidnapped, shot in the leg and had to jump out of a moving car."

"It was Connelly, wasn't it?"

She nodded. "I was dumb enough to think he was legit when he said he needed to take me in for questioning."

"Dumb has nothing to do with it. He had everyone fooled. I think he wanted to use you to get classified information he could sell to interested third parties."

"Did the police catch him?"

"Yes, you're safe, and I'm really sorry."

She waved away his apology.

"How bad is the gunshot wound?"

"It hit me in the thigh, but the bullet penetrated just below the skin and passed through. No major damage done."

"Thank God. How are you feeling?"

"Not bad, considering. I got a little road rash from jumping out of the car, but it'll heal."

Alex sat down on the edge of the bed. "When I heard you were hurt, I was terrified. I don't think I've ever been so scared in my life."

She laughed. "Don't get all melodramatic on me. I'm okay."

"Seriously, Yasmine. I feel like this is partly my fault."

"You couldn't have known what Connelly was up to."

"I could have if I'd paid more attention. If I'd been less focused on you and more focused on the facts."

"Nobody's perfect."

He had to tell her. She had to know how he felt, how far from right his life was without her. How much he wanted her—more than anything else he'd ever wanted.

"Yasmine, please give me another chance." He didn't care if he had to beg. He'd get on his knees if that's what it took.

A stricken look crossed her face, and she quickly subdued it. He'd hurt her, no doubt, and he had no right to expect forgiveness.

"I've wanted you since the first moment I laid eyes on you. Can we start all over again, take things slow, follow all the relationship rules and see what happens?"

She shook her head, and Alex felt his one true chance at lasting happiness slipping through his fingers. "Trust me, once you've started breaking the rules, it's hard to go back."

"You did. You turned your life around."

"But I never wanted to take it slow with you. That's just not the kind of relationship we could have."

"Why can't we try?"

She closed her eyes for a moment, and he found himself mesmerized by the lush black quarter moons of lashes resting on her cheeks. When she opened her eyes again, he could see they were damp with tears.

"I'm sorry. You'll always be that guy on the witness stand to me. You'll always be a reminder of the worst time of my life, and I don't want that. I paid for my crimes. I don't want you in my life haunting me forever."

Her words were a punch to his gut. One he should have seen coming, one that he had to sit and take like a man. He never should have expected anything more. And she was right—she didn't deserve to have a ghost haunting her for the rest of her life.

"I'm sorry you feel that way." He leaned over and placed a kiss on her cheek, then took her hand in his and kissed it too.

A doctor stuck his head in the doorway. "The nurse will be in to release you in just a few."

"Can I give you a ride home?" Alex asked when the doctor disappeared.

She shook her head. "I'll take a cab."

"So. I guess this is goodbye."

Yasmine nodded, and he couldn't look again to see the tears in her eyes.

YASMINE STARED DOWN at the big stack of romantic comedies Cass had just plopped on the coffee table and felt her stomach twist into a knot. She understood her friend's intentions—after yesterday, it was a safe bet Yasmine wouldn't want to watch any shoot-'em-up action flicks. But she'd left out the little detail of her telling Alex to get lost last night.

It was New Year's Eve, she was recovering from a kidnapping, a gunshot wound and the most horrible breakup of her life, and she was so not in the mood for merrily ringing in the New Year.

"I don't think I can watch any of those," she said.

Cass sighed. "Oh, come on, I know you're not crazy about Renee Zellweger, but the guys in these movies are hot."

"It's just the whole notion of romance that I'm not crazy about tonight."

"What happened? I *thought* Alex was suspiciously missing from the scene."

He was the last person she wanted to talk about. "What about Drew?"

Cass shot her a look. "How about we agree not to talk men until we've had at least three margaritas?"

"I can't drink because of the painkillers the hospital gave me."

"Okay, so let's not talk men until *I've* had at least three cocktails."

"Can't we just skip the whole subject of men?" Yasmine asked as she eyed the grocery bag Cass had brought over.

She followed her friend as Cass carried the bag to the kitchen.

"Don't tell me Alex is the one who shot you."

"God, no! Of course not. If you must know, I broke it off permanently with him, and it wasn't pretty. End of subject."

"No fair. You can't drop a little bomb like that without telling more."

Yasmine ignored her, putting the margarita mix in the

fridge and opening the bags of jalapeño chips and chocolate chip cookies to dump in bowls.

"Okay fine. You want to know what happened with Drew? He told me he wants us to date exclusively. After less than a week!"

"That's great."

"No, it's crazy. I froze, and then he felt stupid, and then I said I thought we were just having fun, and he said he didn't think we should see each other anymore."

"Cass!"

"I know. I feel really bad for hurting him."

"You could still call and apologize, maybe explain that you don't have the emotional wiring of a normal human being."

"I already used that explanation. He wasn't buying it."

"He must have been really into you."

"After a week? That's crazy."

"Don't you believe in whirlwind romance and love at first sight?"

"Hell, no. I mean, I loved David Lee Roth at first sight, and look how that turned out."

"Falling for rock stars on MTV doesn't count."

"All that whirlwind romance stuff, it's just kind of a convenient notion, you know?"

"No, I don't know." But she did. She wasn't even sure why she was arguing this point when she'd never experienced the mythical concept herself.

"It's the kind of thing romance novelists probably made up to suit their plots. Dashing hero falls in love at first sight with spitfire heroine, but spitfire heroine is too busy saving her daddy's ranch to be bothered with love—that is, until the evil cattle-rustling villain comes along and shows her that having a dashing hero around the ranch wouldn't be such a bad idea. And it all happens within the space of two weeks."

"You're sounding more jaded than usual, you know."

And yet Yasmine was feeling just as jaded as Cass sounded, just as beaten down by her love life and confused and not sure what the hell she wanted anymore.

"You're the one who can't bear to watch a romantic comedy."

Yasmine eased down onto the couch, doing her best not to strain the bullet wound, and stared at the decorating show that was nearing its big room-makeover climax. It was a rerun, one she'd seen and therefore knew ended with the homeowners ecstatic with their mod-style living room. She couldn't remember the last time she'd gotten so excited over something as this couple was about to be over their new lime-green lamps.

"How did our lives get so dismal?" she said.

Cass finished chewing the cookie she'd shoved into her mouth whole before she answered. "It's called self-pity. We don't have anyone to blame but ourselves if we're not happy."

"But we should be happy. I mean, we're young. We have good jobs, we're healthy, blah blah blah…"

"Aside from the fact that you were just shot and kidnapped, you're life's pretty much perfect."

"Thanks for the reminder."

"And do you really love that dull-as-hell job of yours?"

Yasmine ignored the question and turned her attention to the jalapeño chips, which were a far easier subject than her career aspirations or lack thereof.

"Do you? I mean, look at you. You've got enough

brains for two people, but instead of using what you've got, you settle for a job that has absolutely no chance of ever taking advantage of all your talent."

"I've got a great job."

"You work for a company that makes games with titles like Bodice Ripper. You've got a decent job for a new college grad, but given your talent, you should have been thinking of moving up and out by now."

Yasmine shoved chips into her mouth and pretended to watch the closing credits of the decorating show. She couldn't deal with her wrecked love life, her kidnapping trauma and her apparent lack of ambition all in one conversation.

"Bodice Ripper is actually a pretty funny game, you know. Did you try out that copy I gave you?"

"No."

"It's just like the old-school romance novels we were talking about. Hot hero, busty heroine, kinky bad guy… And you get points every time your hero needs to rip his own shirt off, and double points if he rips the heroine's dress off and ravishes her."

"You're avoiding the subject."

"I thought you came over here to cheer me up after my ordeal."

Cass sighed. "Oh, God, I'm sorry. I'm being a total bitch."

"You're really bothered by this whole Drew thing, aren't you?"

"I guess I'm just trying to distract myself from it."

"By focusing on my failures. Thanks a bunch."

"Why don't I put in one of these movies so I can stop talking."

"I'd rather watch *Dream Kitchen*. It's coming on next."

"What is it with you and these home-improvement shows? I don't get the appeal."

"I'm fascinated, that's all. Everything on these shows is so normal and domestic. And there's always a happy ending."

"Of course there's a happy ending. The biggest conflict is whether to mix stripes and prints."

Yasmine realized for the first time that she loved the banal domesticity of these shows, loved the glimpses into a glossy version of everyday America's home life, loved the makeovers of kids' bedrooms, the family rooms remade to accommodate adults, children and pets—the sort of thing that had not happened in her home growing up.

Her toys had been relegated to her room, which had been decorated in a tasteful botanical theme more suited for a grown-up's room than a kid's. That's how her mother had wanted it. Her brilliant, ambitious mother, who had been so determined not to let having a child sidetrack her from her career or her vision of a perfect home.

God, all this time, she'd just been trying not to become her mother….

And if she engaged in another minute of this angst-ridden navel gazing, she was going to have to find a gun and shoot herself in another major body part.

Cass had put a movie in the DVD player, and now she was flipping through the bonus material with the remote.

"Are you really going to subject me to this? Maybe we should just play a board game or something."

"Don't even suggest it. I know you only own Trivial Pursuit."

"But I just got the newest edition from my parents and haven't tried it out yet!"

"Forget it. We're watching the movie," she said, staring straight ahead at the TV with grim determination.

"Am I really that obnoxious when I play?"

"I'm not going to answer that."

Yasmine sighed and curled up on the couch, resigned to her romantic-comedy fate. She had to admit, Renee Zellwegger did have a certain squinty-eyed charm, and a half hour into the movie, she was starting to buy the message that love could solve all of life's bigger problems.

"Do you think I screwed up dumping Alex?" she dared to ask.

"The more important question is, do *you* think you screwed up?"

"What if he was my one and only shot at true love or something?"

"I think you of all people have at least a couple of shots at true love."

"But what if he was the one shot I was supposed to make?"

Cass glanced over at her. "If you believe that, then why did you break up with him?"

"I broke up because I was scared. I thought he'd always remind me of being a convict."

"Hmm. I guess that's true," she said, sounding more interested in the movie than Yasmine's plight.

"That was not the voice of sincerity."

Cass grabbed the remote and hit the pause button. "You're the one who's always talking about the importance of accepting yourself for what you are. So what if he reminds you of your past? At least you know he doesn't have any issues with it."

"Is that part of the reason you didn't want to get serious with Drew? You didn't want to tell him about your stripper years."

"We're talking about your screwed-up love life here, not mine."

On the paused TV screen, the heroine was frozen in the middle of a lonely New Year's Eve crying jag. Bizarrely appropriate.

"So what are your New Year's resolutions?"

"No more sex with nerdy guys who don't know the deal about me and my romance-free lifestyle."

"Would you stop calling Drew a nerd. He's just a little offbeat. He doesn't try to be cool, which in my book is a definite plus."

"What's your resolution? No more gorgeous, available, perfect men?"

"Alex is *not* perfect. Remember, I didn't even know his name was Alex until a few days ago!"

"So he testified against you and sent you to a juvie center. Is that really so awful?"

"No, but it's pretty damn bad that he slept with me just to find out if I was still doing anything illegal."

"Come on, Yasmine. You know that's not the whole truth—the man's got an overly guilty conscience. He slept with you because he was hot for you, plain and simple."

"And because it was a convenient way to gain my trust."

"Seriously, have you ever met a guy who wanted sex for any other reason than simply because it's his favorite thing to do?"

"That's beside the point."

"No, it *is* the point. You've got to stop letting this whole investigation thing bother you. If he got it up, it's because he wanted to sleep with you. No other reason."

Was Cass right? Yasmine wondered. Had she been too hard on Alex, and had he been too hard on himself? She thought of his otherwise strict sense of honor and realized just how right Cass was.

"Oh, hell."

"You know I'm right."

Yes, she did. And she felt like a fool.

"Do you think I've screwed up for good with him?"

"There's only one way to find out."

"What about you? Are you really going to mope your way through the New Year?"

"Do you have another suggestion?"

"You're clearly unhappy with the Drew situation. Why don't you at least open yourself up to possibilities? Maybe you'd be blissfully happy with him if you gave him a chance."

"Or not."

"Why don't you offer him some sort of alternative arrangement—like sex with the possibility of something more."

Cass was silent. Finally she said, "What if he's horrified that I used to be a stripper?"

"Then he sucks, but there's only one way to find out."

She sighed. "I guess I've gone this far. I've already entered the complication zone. I'll always wonder what might have been if I don't give it a shot."

"Should we go find our men?" Yasmine asked.

"I think we have to. It's either that or sit here feeling sorry for ourselves on the most important night of the year."

They were off the couch and scrambling for shoes and coats, and in less than a minute they were both ready to go.

They opened the door, and Yasmine was stepping out into the hallway when she spotted Alex. He was standing holding a bottle of champagne, looking contrite and gorgeous.

Cass looked at her and smiled. "I'll be going now," she said. "Happy New Year!"

And with that she was running down the stairs and out the door, leaving Yasmine and Alex standing there, silent, staring at each other.

"Call me optimistic," he finally said, "but I was sitting home alone, trying to figure out what to do with myself, and I realized the only thing I wanted to do was come here and beg you to give me another chance."

She wanted to play it cool, remain a little stoic, but she got all teary-eyed again instead.

"You'd better come inside," she said.

_17_

CASS GLANCED AT THE CLOCK glowing green on her dash. She still had time. She'd gone home, changed clothes and grabbed her old portable stereo loaded with her favorite dance CD. Now she was parked in Drew's driveway, trying to muster her nerve to get out of the car. If he was home, they could maybe ring in the New Year together.

If she was lucky.

Mere groveling might not be good enough. She'd have to take extreme measures, possibly, and she was prepared. She hadn't realized how badly she wanted to see him again until she'd set her mind to the task.

With her insides trembling, she got out of the car, carried her stereo and some clothes in a duffle bag up the sidewalk, rang the doorbell and waited. Seconds passed, and she rang again just to be sure he'd heard. Then she breathed a sigh of relief to hear footsteps from inside the house.

When the door opened, Drew was standing on the other side, his glasses missing, his hair disheveled and his chest bare.

"I'm sorry, did I interrupt something?" she asked, feeling foolish for not considering the possibility that he'd already have a woman with him.

"Actually, yes," he said without betraying any emotion. "You woke me up."

"Could you please let me in for a minute so we can talk?"

"No."

"Okay, we can talk like this. I just want to say I'm sorry, and that I want to give us a chance. I may not be all that open to romance, but I'd like to at least be open to possibilities with you. So maybe we could, you know, keep having sex…and see what happens."

"I don't really see the point now," he said.

"Would it make a difference if I were naked?" she said, setting her bag on the sidewalk.

His gaze dropped to her leopard-print trench coat. "It would be slightly more entertaining, but no, I can't see how it would make a difference."

"Let's try it," she said as she opened her coat and revealed the skimpy ensemble she wore beneath.

Her body-skimming leopard-print baby doll barely covered a black lace bra and panties. And her bare legs led down to a pair of black stiletto heels.

The damp night air was cold. Damn cold. Her nipples turned to pebbles when she let the coat fall open.

Drew glanced around the neighborhood, then back at her. "Cover yourself up!" he stage-whispered.

"Why? Worried that your neighbors will see me?"

Cass had hidden for too long behind lies that never hinted at the dancing she'd earned her living on for so many years. She didn't miss stripping—okay, well, she did occasionally miss the empowerment it gave her.

She missed the raw, female power she had over every man in a room when she stepped out onto a stage and wrapped her leg around the pole.

But she'd finished that chapter of her life and didn't

intend to go back. She didn't want to dwell on the mistakes she'd made or the people she'd hurt when she'd been young and reckless. She had other ways of commanding power now.

Yet she did want Drew to know all of her and accept her for who she was and who she had been. If he couldn't accept her, he wasn't worth any more of her time.

"Please let me in. I have to show you something, and I don't want you to say anything until I'm finished, okay?"

"Um, okay," he said, sounding perplexed as he stepped aside.

She entered the apartment and looked around to make sure she had enough room to dance. Definitely enough space for a one-woman show.

"You'll want to sit down for this," she said, and he did, easing down onto the edge of the couch as if he might need to hop up again and flee the room at any moment.

She placed the portable stereo on his dining room table and hit the play button for the CD that was already cued up. The music started, and she let her coat slide off her shoulders and onto the floor, where she kicked it aside.

Cass had always understood the power of focusing her dance on a specific guy, making him believe he was the only one in the room she was taking her clothes off for. So she did. As she started to dance, her body moving as if making love, her gaze locked on Drew, she could read the emotions playing across his face.

Interest, confusion, arousal, mistrust and, finally, appreciation. He sat back a little, continuing to watch as she removed the baby doll, sliding it over her shoulders, down her waist, over her hips and legs.

She kicked it aside, then did a little spin as she unlatched her bra, opened her arms and flung it aside. As she danced before Drew, her chest bare, she felt as if she'd just bared something more. As if she was showing him her heart, opening up that place where he could hurt her the most, and where there also might be the greatest potential for pleasure.

And that, she realized, was the reason she'd run scared before. Her heart had been telling her she didn't just want sex with this man. She wanted to see what else might happen. In spite of her happy life, for once she actually wanted the complications.

Finally she hooked her thumbs into the sides of her panties and shimmied them down over her hips, let them fall to her feet, met Drew's gaze and held it as she slid her hands over her torso and breasts.

She worked her hips, lowered herself like a cat to the floor, crawled toward Drew and then twirled onto her back, where she ended the dance with her legs crossed in the air.

When the song stopped and the room was silent again, she could hear his steady breathing, but for a few moments he said nothing.

Then finally, "Wow."

"Did you like it?"

"You dance like a pro."

She pushed herself up to a sitting position and rested her arms on his knees in front of her.

"The truth is, I worked my way through college by stripping."

Drew stared at her, slack-jawed, and didn't say a word.

She took a deep breath and kept going. "I was Cassi, with an *i*, and I could work a pole like nobody's business."

"That's why you don't like me calling you Cassie?"

She nodded. "I'm tired of hiding my past. If you don't like it, then I'm definitely not the girl for you."

"Let me get this straight. You were an exotic dancer, and you're afraid I wouldn't like that?"

"Yeah."

"Come here," he said, pulling her into his lap.

"Is this close enough?"

"Barely," he said, taking a long, appreciative look at her bare breasts. "I just want you to know, I've never met a woman like you before."

"You mean, a former stripper?"

"I mean, a woman as fun, exciting, intelligent and sexy as you."

"Aren't you a little bothered that I used to take my clothes off for a living?"

He slid his hands up her torso and around to her backside. "I don't give a damn. You have an amazing body, and what you've done with it is your own business. If you were okay with being a stripper, then I'm okay with it."

"I guess that's the problem. I've always felt a little ashamed of that part of my life."

"Ashamed why?"

"Lots of reasons. I didn't treat myself very well, let men treat me badly, too, made some mistakes…"

"Nobody has a perfect past. Whatever has happened to you, has made you the woman you are today, and I'm interested in that woman."

"There's something else," she said before she could lose her nerve. "I turn forty next month."

"So?" He stared blankly at her.

"I just thought you should know. Some people have been led to believe I'm slightly younger than forty," she said casually.

"Okay."

"And also, I'm not quite ready for that going-steady stuff. I was hoping, maybe, you'd be interested in picking up where we left off, and…"

"And just having sex?"

"Just seeing what happens."

He gave the matter some thought. "I can live with that."

Cass tried to speak, but her throat tightened up, and all she could do was kiss Drew. She wrapped her arms around him and kissed him for all she was worth, until they both had to come up for air.

Finally she found her voice. "I'm sorry for making this so hard."

"It's okay, so long as you're going to stay here and ring in the New Year with me."

"There's no place else I'd rather be," she said.

He smiled his crooked smile, and Cass knew that wherever their affair took them, she wanted to go. She wanted to explore the possibilities, follow the adventure and find out if there was a chance for happily ever after.

YASMINE OPENED THE WINDOW so they could have a better view of the fireworks when the clock struck midnight. Then she turned to Alex and expelled a shaky sigh. He'd just finished pouring glasses of champagne for them, but she'd forgotten to tell him she couldn't drink alcohol with her pain medication.

Now when she looked at him, she could see past the surface changes to the man he'd been years ago, sitting on the witness stand. He didn't look so different, after all. And the questions remained. Could she totally forgive him, and could she really live with the reminder of her sins every day? Could she trust that he saw past her surface?

Okay, she was definitely getting ahead of herself there. Who knew if Alex would want a future with her beyond tomorrow, or next week?

In the black sky, a starburst of red lit the darkness, followed by more glittering bursts of white and blue. The bangs and whistles of the fireworks reminded Yasmine of a New Year's Eve she'd once spent in Paris as a kid with her parents. And the thought of her parents made her wonder, for the first time, what they would think of Alex if they ever met him.

Would they like him? Would her father talk to him about rugby, and would her mother size him up and deem him acceptable? It didn't matter to her one way or the other, but, she realized now, they would like him. He was the kind of guy parents wanted their daughters to end up with—upright, strong, intelligent, handsome....

He may have tried to give himself to the dark side in pursuing her, but even then he'd had an honorable motive.

She smiled and glanced over at Alex with a little pang of wistfulness for reasons she couldn't put a finger on, but when his gaze met hers, she saw something unexpectedly intense there.

He wasn't smiling, and he didn't look at all as though he was enjoying the merriment of the holiday.

"What's up?" Yasmine asked.

He pulled her closer and rested his hands at the small

of her back. "I'm still waiting to find out if you'll forgive me."

She expelled a pent-up breath and took his hands in hers. "I do forgive you, and what I said earlier at the hospital—I was speaking under duress."

"Meaning?"

"I wasn't thinking too clearly, but now I realize, it doesn't matter if you remind me of the past. I want to know about the future—I want to know what comes next for us."

He smiled a tentative smile, and for the first time Yasmine realized how vulnerable he was, waiting for her to come around. "We haven't talked about what comes next," he said.

"I don't know."

A burst of light in the sky lit up Alex's face for a moment, and Yasmine was afraid of what she saw. He was about to say something she was pretty sure she didn't want to hear.

"I want there to be a 'next.' A next day, a next month, a next year, a next lifetime."

Yasmine's throat closed up, and she made an insensible sound.

"Are you okay?" he asked.

She opened her mouth to speak, but nothing came out.

"You have to know I love you, don't you?"

She wanted to shut him up with a kiss, make the whole discussion just stop right there, sealed in time, before things could go bad. But time never stopped. Through the good and the bad, it marched forward, and so she joined the march with the only thing she could say.

"I love you, too."

He smiled. "We should do something about that, don't you think?"

"Like what?"

"I can't imagine my life without you. I've wanted you since the first time I saw you a decade ago."

Yasmine's breath caught. He'd wanted her all this time. He'd wanted her, and he'd testified against her. She tried to imagine his inner turmoil, and then she realized, this was why he hadn't fought his termination from the FBI. Because of her and his overblown sense of honor.

It was the most romantic thing she'd ever heard. And the craziest.

"You gave up your FBI career because of me."

"It doesn't matter."

"It does. You should have fought for it."

"I'd rather have you."

"I'm not worth losing a career over."

"You're the most fascinating woman I've ever known, and there's some kind of special connection between us—you have to feel it, too."

She did. There was no denying they were soul mates.

"I want you more than anything," he said, and they were the words she'd been waiting all her life to hear.

"Anyway you want me, you've got me," she said, and she melted into him.

Had she ever been wanted so completely? Had she ever been the most desired thing in a person's life?

She couldn't say she had, and she couldn't imagine a better feeling in the world now that she knew she was.

Epilogue

Five Months Later

YASMINE HAD BEEN BREATHING paint fumes for the past few days, and now she liked to think she'd become immune to their side effects. That they were no longer killing off her brain cells one by one.

"Nice work," Alex said from behind her, startling her out of what was likely a paint-fume-induced stupor. "I can't believe you've already finished the whole room."

She turned to see him admiring the shade of gray blue she'd just painted their front office. DiCarlo Consulting and Investigations' new business office officially opened tomorrow, though they already had enough clients to keep them busy for several months.

Yasmine had been freaked out at first by the idea of going into business with Alex, doing independent security consulting and investigations. But once she settled into the idea, she knew it was exactly the change she'd needed.

The sex game industry had been fun, but she wanted a different challenge, and she loved the idea of working closely with her soon-to-be husband.

People had warned her about working with a spouse, but she couldn't think of anyone else she'd rather be with all day. They needed to make up for lost time.

"I didn't want you to think I'd grown soft during those two weeks in the South Pacific."

They'd taken a vacation together last month, a cruise during which Alex had proposed to her. Those blissful days and nights aboard the ship and in Tahiti had been two of the best weeks of Yasmine's life, but what she'd been looking forward to most was now. The everyday routines together, the day-to-day humdrum life. She'd had enough of excitement, and she'd traveled enough to last her a while. What she'd never had, and what she craved, was this closeness, this intimacy that came only with living your life with another person.

They hadn't picked a wedding date yet, but it didn't matter to Yasmine. She'd already given herself to Alex heart and soul. The formal part could wait a few months.

"What I think is, you're working too damn hard. You need to save your energy for me."

"Oh?" She turned and slipped her hands around his waist and up the hard planes of his back.

"I'm a man with certain needs, you know."

"Believe me, I know." Every night, he had needs—needs she loved fulfilling.

He dipped his head down to kiss her, and she felt him grow hard against her abdomen. A few feet away, the soon-to-be receptionist's desk sat covered in a drop cloth, the perfect destination for them.

"I'll just close these blinds," Alex said, letting go of her for a moment.

"Is the door locked?"

"Yep, just locked it."

"So you had no intention of helping me clean up

when you came in here," she said as he lifted her onto the desk and nestled between her legs.

"Well, I did, but then I saw you bent over that paint can, and—"

"You're so predictable."

"I'll do all the clean-up," he said, "if you'll do me."

Afternoon sex breaks were definitely an unexpected and most welcome benefit of working together.

* * * * *

Look for Jamie Sobrato's next book,
ONCE UPON A SEDUCTION.
Coming in January 2006 from Harlequin Blaze!

MAKE YOUR HOLIDAYS *Sizzle*!

SAVE $1.⁰⁰

WHEN YOU PURCHASE ANY
2 HARLEQUIN BLAZE TITLES

U.S. RETAILERS: Harlequin Enterprises Ltd. will pay the face value of this coupon plus 8¢ if submitted by customer for this product only. Any other use constitutes fraud. Coupon is nonassignable. Void if taxed, prohibited or restricted by law. Consumer must pay any government taxes. Void if copied. For reimbursement submit coupons and proof of sales directly to Harlequin Enterprises Ltd., P.O. Box 880478, El Paso, TX 88588-0478, U.S.A. Cash value 1/100¢.

Coupon valid from October 15, 2005, to December 31, 2005.
Redeemable at participating retail outlets.
Limit one coupon per purchase.

11201

5 65373 00076 2   (8100) 0 11201

With six new titles every month, these red-hot reads
are sure to spice things up this holiday season!

HARLEQUIN® *Blaze*

MAKE YOUR HOLIDAYS *Sizzle*!

SAVE $1.⁰⁰

WHEN YOU PURCHASE ANY
2 HARLEQUIN BLAZE TITLES

With six new titles every month, these red-hot reads are sure to spice things up this holiday season!

HBCPN1105C